"One of the reasons I'm still a stupid virgin is because of you!"

All the anger seemed to melt from his face as a tender expression took over. "I don't think there's anything stupid about being a virgin in this day and age," he said softly. "But since I've spoilt you for any other man so far, then the least I can do is undo the damage I've done."

"What...what do you mean?"

"I mean, Angie, my sweet," he said, kissing her lightly on the lips, "that you're quite right. It is high time you lost your virginity, but I also think your first experience should be with someone you really fancy.... Therefore I'm volunteering to be your first lover."

Dear Reader,

Love can be full of surprises!

Welcome to the first book in Miranda Lee's bewitching trilogy AFFAIRS TO REMEMBER. This month, and for the next two months, this popular Australian author brings you three complete stories of love affairs with a difference—there are twists to all the tales that you won't forget.

Read on now to find out how one stolen kiss changed Angie's life forever...!

Sincerely,

The Editor

MIRANDA LEE

A Kiss to Remember

Harlequin Books

TORONTO • NEW YORK • LONDON
AMSTERDAM • PARIS • SYDNEY • HAMBURG
STOCKHOLM • ATHENS • TOKYO • MILAN
MADRID • WARSAW • BUDAPEST • AUCKLAND

ISBN 0-373-11849-X

A KISS TO REMEMBER

First North American Publication 1996.

CHAPTER ONE

ANGIE looked over at the sulky-faced girl sitting on the other side of her desk and shook her head sadly. What was the world coming to when girls thought they were freaks just because they were still virgins at seventeen?

'Debbie, dear,' Angie said, with as much patience as she could muster at five to four on a Friday afternoon. 'It is not a crime *not* to be sexually active at your age. In fact, in view of the health hazards these days, I would say it was very sensible. Can't you at least wait till you leave school? This year is almost over, after all. You have less than twelve months to go before you graduate.'

Which could be part of the problem, Angie suspected. Next year—Debbie's final year—would be a very stressful one. A lot of Year Eleven students let their hair down at this time of the year. This year's exams were over, summer had arrived, and the end-of-year party scene had well and truly begun—with all the accompanying hazards of alcohol and drugs. A lot of girls lost their virginity at such times, but mostly this was an unpremeditated event. Debbie's decision to sleep with her boyfriend was hardly that.

'Look, I know you probably think you're madly in love with this boy,' Angie went on. 'But love rarely lasts long at your age. Next year—or even next term—it will probably be another boy, then another. If you sleep with all of them, then...'

'I'm not at all in love with Warren,' Debbie denied, her defiant eyes shocking Angie. 'I just want to know what it's like, that's all. You read so much about it and everyone else is doing it.'

'Everyone else is *not* doing it!' Angie argued, her cheeks pinkening with what she hoped looked like indignation.

'That's all very well for you to say, Miss. I'll bet you know what it's like. I'll bet you've had loads of boyfriends!'

Angie could feel her face beginning to burn. 'Now, you look here, young lady,' she began firmly. 'My boyfriends are *my* business. What we are here to discuss is *your* sex-life, not mine! Besides, I happen to be twenty-four years old—not seventeen. Believe me when I tell you that when I was your age I definitely was a virgin.'

And you still are, a small dark voice pointed out drily in her head.

Angie scowled, both at the voice and at Debbie.

'As your school counsellor,' she continued, in her best lecturing tone, 'my advice to you is to wait till you are at least in a steady relationship before you take this step. Making love should not be an experiment—especially the first time. It should be a very special experience between two people who truly care about one another. It should be an experience to remember and look back on with good feelings, not regret.'

Even as she was saying the words Angie could see she was not getting through to the girl. Debbie confirmed this opinion by pouting and not meeting her eyes. 'Rebecca said you'd understand,' the girl grumbled. 'She said you'd help me like you did her.'

'Rebecca was an entirely different case,' Angie muttered, even as she knew she was defeated. Privately, she might be a romantic and an idealist. Professionally, she was a realist.

As Debbie's counsellor she had a responsibility to look after the girl's physical as well as her mental health. For they were intrinsically linked. Unhappily, she opened the bottom drawer and drew out a couple of condoms from the supply of samples she kept there, ready to be given out with discretion to any girl over the age of consent who came to her with a similar attitude to Debbie's.

'I am giving you these most reluctantly, Debbie, and only because you seem determined to do this. They are not my way of condoning your decision, or giving you permission, but I can't in all conscience see you without protection. Some young men aren't too caring about young women who give themselves to them without love,' she finished pointedly.

At last, Debbie had the good grace to blush. 'I didn't realise you were so old-fashioned,' she muttered. 'Rebecca said you were real cool.'

'You think it's cool to be promiscuous?' Angie asked sharply.

'No. But I think it's stupid to be ignorant about sex,' she flung back.

Angie stiffened.

Debbie stood up and went to leave, then stopped, glancing anxiously over her shoulder at Angie. 'You . . . you won't tell my parents, will you?'

'No. You're over the legal age of consent.'

The girl suddenly smiled at her. 'Thanks, Miss. And I promise to think about everything you said. See you next Monday!' And she fairly skipped out of the door.

Angie stayed sitting at her desk for a few minutes, gnawing away at her bottom lip and wondering if Debbie was right. Maybe she *was* impossibly old-fashioned. And impossibly romantic. And impossibly cautious.

Was it silly of her to wait for Mr Right to come along before she made love? Naïve of her to want to see stars when a man kissed her before she let him go further? Stupid of her to hope that it wouldn't end up a matter of making a conscious choice to go to bed with a man—to believe she would be so madly, blindly and irrevocably in love that it would just happen quite naturally!

'Yes, yes, yes!' her flatmate answered to all three questions, when Angie posed them to her as they drove home together that afternoon.

Angie remained unconvinced. Vanessa was thirty years old and a terrible cynic about men and love. A maths and science teacher at the same girls' school where Angie was the school counsellor, she was a striking-looking though brittle brunette, who frightened most men off with her superior intelligence and incisive wit. Which was a shame because, basically, Vanessa liked men a lot.

They'd been colleagues at the same private girls' school for nearly a year, but had only been flatting together for a couple of months, Angie's previous flatmate having left to go overseas. This was the first time Angie had really opened up to the older woman about her personal life. And, to give Vanessa credit, she accepted the news of her inexperience without too much shock, though she was typically cutting in her advice.

'For pity's sake, go out and get yourself laid before it's too late. How can you possibly counsel all those randy little teenagers who come to you for advice if you don't have any first-hand knowledge of the subject? Good Lord, Angie, if you wait for Mr Right these days, you might go to your grave a virgin! Frankly, I can't understand how a girl who looks like you do made it through her teenage years without scores of horny boys jumping on your bones every five minutes!'

'I didn't say they didn't try...'

'And there wasn't one you fancied back?' Vanessa's tone was sheer scepticism.

An image swept into Angie's mind. Of brilliant blue eyes and flashing white teeth, of windswept fair hair and golden-bronze skin, of a face like a Greek God and a body to match.

'There was one,' she admitted.

'Only *one*?' Vanessa squawked.

Angie smiled ruefully to herself. 'Believe me, after Lance, no other male has ever measured up.'

Which had always been the problem, hadn't it? Angie realised with sudden insight. Once you'd tasted ambrosia it was hard to settle for plain bread. She'd always told herself that her shrinking from casual sex had been because of that AIDS chap, who'd come to her high school and lectured them upon the dangers of such activities.

But it hadn't been that at all, Angie finally conceded. It was because subconsciously she'd compared every boy and then every man she met to Lance Sterling. And they'd all come up wanting.

'He sounds awfully intriguing,' Vanessa said.

'Intriguing,' Angie repeated thoughtfully. 'Yes, one could say that about him. Among other things.'

'Do tell. I'm dying of curiosity already.'

Angie frowned, aware that thoughts of Lance had been teasing her mind a lot this past week. Mostly because tonight was her brother's thirtieth birthday party, which she would be obliged to attend.

Anything to do with Bud always reminded her of Lance.

Not that her brother had anything much to do with Lance these days. Their once close friendship had waned after Lance married four years ago and moved to Melbourne to live. It had now come down to exchanging Christmas cards once a year.

Not that they'd ever had much in common, except for doing the same business degree at the same university in Sydney. Angie had never been able to work out exactly what Lance had seen in Bud—and vice versa. They had come from two entirely different worlds. They'd had two entirely different personalities.

Perhaps it had been the old case of an attraction of opposites. Or perhaps it had just amused Lance to have a simple country boy as a friend, whom he could impress with his sophistication and wealth. As it had amused him to impress his friend's simple country sister that fateful summer nine years ago...

CHAPTER TWO

ANGIE sat on the top step of the front veranda, waiting impatiently for her brother to arrive with his exciting-sounding friend. Bud had said in his last letter that they'd be leaving Sydney straight after breakfast. But it was a five-hour drive north up to Wilga, then another twenty minutes out to the farm. Since it was only ten to twelve, they probably wouldn't be here for at least another hour.

Still, Angie couldn't seem to settle to anything else. So she stayed where she was, anxiously watching the valley road and hoping against hope that they'd started out earlier than intended.

For the millionth time that morning she wondered what this Lance looked like.

Bud had said in his letters that his friend was very good-looking. But Bud's idea of good-looking and Angie's idea of good-looking were often poles apart. Their views on things differed as vastly as did their own looks.

Bud took after their mother, who was small and dark, with black wavy hair, chocolate-brown eyes and an inclination to put on weight easily. Angie, however, was a female version of their father—tall and athletically slim, with auburn hair and widely spaced green eyes.

Their natures were different as well. Bud was easily bored, and craved excitement and companionship all the time. Angie was far more placid and private. She was quite happy with her own company, liking nothing better than to go riding by herself, or to curl up all alone on her bed to write poetry or read a book. She liked to think rather than talk. Bud could talk underwater, like their mother.

A cloud of dust in the distance had Angie jumping to her feet, her hand hooding her eyes from the sunlight as she peered down the hill. A car was coming along the valley road, going as fast as her heart was suddenly beating.

It was Bud and his friend. She was sure of it.

Somewhere at the back of her mind Angie knew she was acting totally out of character, getting excited over a member of the opposite sex. Especially one she hadn't met yet.

She was not boy-mad, as were most other girls in her class. Her classmates actually thought her shy.

She let them think it.

Angie knew that she wasn't really shy. Just reserved. She liked her personal space and hated being harassed in any way. Unwanted male attention sometimes embarrassed and always annoyed her. Frankly, she found most boys at school exceedingly adolescent, noisy and irritating. She'd actually been relieved by her father's edict a couple of years back that she could not have a boyfriend till she was sixteen. It was the perfect excuse for her to turn down the invitations she received from her over-eager admirers.

And there were many. For Angie was a very attractive girl. In the past few months some people had started using the word 'beautiful'.

Yet she never made any attempt to enhance her looks or look older, as some girls might have. She never used make-up, always wore her long straight hair up in a simple ponytail, and was happiest wearing jeans or shorts, plus one of her father's shirts.

Today was no different. Angie had too much common sense to try to attract someone like Bud's friend from Sydney. He was twenty-two, after all— one year older than Bud—and wouldn't look twice at a fifteen-year-old girl. On top of that he was very, very rich—the only son and heir of one of Sydney's wealthiest families.

Perhaps it was this last factor that Angie found so fascinating. She'd never met any really rich people before, and the things Bud had told her about Lance's home and lifestyle sounded very glamorous. Totally different from the simple country life the Browns led.

Angie had been amazed to hear that after finishing high school Lance had travelled the world for a whole year before starting uni. He and Bud had not become friends till this last year, and no doubt now that their degrees were finished their paths would soon diverge. Next year Bud would have to go out into the real world and find himself a job, whereas Lance would be automatically given a cushy executive position in one of the family's companies.

Sterling Industries had many fingers in many pies—from food and cleaning products to furniture, from plastics to various mining interests. Apparently, Lance had offered to find Bud a job, but Bud had refused, and Angie was proud of him for that. Not that she was worried about her brother going out on his own in search of a career. Bud had enough drive and energy to succeed in whatever he put his mind to.

The wire door creaked behind her, and Angie turned to see her mother coming out, wiping floury hands on the apron which was doing its best to circumnavigate her rotund middle. Though not yet forty, Nora Brown had long surrendered to her genes, plus her love of food.

Not that she worried about her weight. Nothing ever worried Nora Brown. She was easygoing, easy to please and easy to love. If she had a fault it was her tendency to be blunt with others at times. She was not rude, just a little tactless on occasion. Still, everyone loved her—especially her husband, Morris.

A very handsome man, Morris Brown could have had his pick of any number of local girls. He'd chosen Nora, who was short, plump, dark, and very ordinary-looking.

It was a tribute to Nora's totally natural self-esteem that she had never found this in any way amazing. She accepted Morris's love as her due, and loved him back with all the love in her ample bosom. Twenty-two years later, they still adored each other.

'Did I hear a car coming?' Nora asked hopefully.

'Flying, more like it,' Angie said.

Her mother stepped forward, dark eyes twinkling, a wide smile on her homely face. 'I'll bet that's my Buddy driving. Dear me, but he's a naughty boy when he gets behind the wheel of a car. I hope his father's still down on the river flats and can't see this.'

The car came into view, sending some gravel flying as it lurched around a corner on its way up the hill to the house. Red and gleaming, it had silver wheels and the top down.

The sounds of its manic approach sent the dogs shooting out from underneath the weatherboard house, barking in force. A motley lot, there was a brown kelpie named Betsie, a blue cattle-dog cross named Fang and a black Labrador who'd been a guide dog reject, suitably called Max, after the hero in *Get Smart*.

'Betsie! Fang! Max!' Nora called out. 'Stop that racket and get yourselves back under the house before you get run over.'

All three dived for cover just as the red Mercedes Sports came to a screeching halt at the bottom of the front steps. It wasn't her brother's Mercedes, Angie knew, since he didn't own a car, but it was Bud behind the wheel all right; she saw that straight away. He was grinning his head off as he glanced down at his watch.

'Made it before noon by a whole thirty seconds!' he exclaimed excitedly, then gave his passenger a smug look. 'You owe me twenty dollars.'

The sound of a rich laugh sent Angie's eyes swinging over to her brother's friend, and her heart just stopped. As she stared his head turned slowly towards them, his hand lifting lazily to comb back his thick blond hair. He tipped up his perfectly sculptured face and set dancing blue eyes upon them, his laughing mouth showing dazzling white teeth and a dimple in his right cheek.

'Hi,' he said. 'I'm Lance.'

'Hi there, Mum,' Bud called out. 'Hope we didn't scare the chooks too much.'

'Yes, sorry about the ruckus, Mrs Brown,' Bud's friend apologised, still smiling that overwhelmingly engaging smile of his. 'Your son here is insane when it comes to winning a bet.'

'That's all right, young man,' Nora returned. 'I already know my Buddy's weaknesses, as well as his strengths. One seems to be picking very nice friends.'

Bud groaned. 'For pity's sake, Mum, don't flatter him. He's already got a head as big as the Sydney Harbour Bridge.'

'I'll flatter whomever I like in my own house, you cheeky pup,' Nora pretended to reproach him. 'Now, get yourself out of that fancy car, come up here and give your old mother a hug. You too, young man. I'm partial to hugs.'

'Coming right up,' Lance chuckled, and with an extraordinary amount of grace and athleticism, leapt out of the car without opening the door, landing on long legs which supported a body as perfect as his face. Angie had an excellent view of it, standing there, encased in hip-hugging jeans and a muscle-moulding white T-shirt. When his legs moved to propel him up the three steps it looked even better.

Lance had been long hugged by the time Bud made it out of the car and up the steps, by which time Lance had turned his attention to Angie.

'Don't tell me *you're* Bud's little sister?' he drawled, those brilliant blue eyes of his narrowing upon her in a way which did incredible things to her insides. Her previously stopped heart was suddenly racing like a quarter horse in full gallop.

'Do I get a hug from you too?' he asked softly, not waiting for permission but immediately taking her in his arms and squeezing her tight.

After a moment's shock, Angie closed her eyes and let the feel of his firm embrace wash through every pore of her body. It was an experience alien to anything she had ever felt before, making her face flush and her legs go to jelly.

Fear that she might slide down his body on to the veranda in a melted heap forced her to hug him back. But when she did so, he pulled her even more tightly against him, making her fiercely aware of the physical differences between males and females. Her breasts were squashed flat against the hard expanse of his broad chest, and there was a vague assortment of lumps and bumps pressing into her lower abdomen.

'You can let her go now,' Bud said, tapping Lance on the shoulder. 'And don't go getting any funny ideas about my sister. She's only fifteen, you know.'

Lance pulled back to hold her at arm's length, his hands still resting lightly on her hips as he looked her over a second time.

'She looks older,' he said, his voice once again having dropped to that low, lazy timbre which sent little shivers running down her spine.

'Who, Angie?' Bud sounded sceptical. 'Nah, she's just tall, the lucky devil.'

'Five foot ten in her bare feet,' her mother piped up proudly. 'Takes after her father. Buddy here takes after me,' she added, tousling her son's black curly head.

'Mum, stop that,' Bud objected. 'And stop calling me Buddy. You know I hate it.'

'You liked it well enough for your first eighteen years, me lad. Don't go letting life in the big city give you airs and graces. You haven't been giving him airs and graces, have you, Lance?'

Finally, Lance's hands slipped from Angie's hips and she gulped a steadying breath. She did her best to look composed but she just knew her cheeks were flaming.

'Not me, Mrs Brown,' he said, looking away from Angie's face at long last.

'Didn't think so. You seem a mighty fine boy— even if you are from a filthy rich family.'

'Mum!' Bud groaned.

'Well, we all know money can spoil children,' his mother stated quite ingenuously. 'But I can see

Lance here has grown up to be a credit to his mum
and dad. Where is it that your parents have gone
to, Lance?'

'Europe, I think, Mrs Brown.'

Nora was taken aback. 'Don't you *know*?'

Lance's shrug was nonchalant. 'They don't like
to be tied down to a schedule. They just go with
the flow.'

'It seems a strange time to go away, just before
Christmas,' Nora muttered, frowning.

Angie had to agree with her. Christmas was for
families.

'Not to worry,' her mother went on, linking arms
with Lance and smiling broadly up at him. 'You're
spending Christmas with us. We'll look after you,
won't we, Angie?'

Vanessa gave a dry chortle. 'I'll bet your mother
wouldn't have made such an offer if she'd known
how her guest wanted the daughter of the house to
look after him. So what happened? How long
before he made a pass? And how did you possibly
resist him? He sounds gorgeous.'

Angie sighed, then slowed for a set of lights,
stopping a little raggedly. 'He didn't make a pass.
Not once. And he stayed with us most of the
summer, right till the end of January.'

'I don't believe it! He was obviously attracted to
you.'

'Yes, I thought so too. And I was besotted with
him. Followed him around like a puppy. Made every
excuse to be wherever he was.'

'Didn't your brother mind that—his kid sister tagging along all the time?'

'No. Our family has always done things together. Bud and Dad spent a lot of time that summer showing Lance how to do country-style things. They taught him how to ride, how to plough, how to shoot. By the end of his stay he could drill a beer can at one hundred yards. It was only natural for me to help. And who else would be stupid enough to stand around putting empty beer cans on fenceposts for hours?'

The lights turned green and Angie eased ahead in the heavy city-going traffic.

'Did your family know you were ga-ga over him?' Vanessa asked.

'I don't think so. As I said before, I've always been a private person. I didn't wear my heart on my sleeve then any more than I do now. Certainly Dad and Bud never guessed. I think maybe Mum might have suspected something, though oddly enough she didn't say anything at the time—which wasn't like her at all. Maybe she was smart enough to see the passing nature of the situation and knew that any comment would have made my eventual agony worse.'

'But Lance knew, didn't he?'

'Oh, yes ... Lance knew ...'

'And how did he feel about you?'

Angie shrugged. 'Who knows? I thought he cared for me. He certainly liked me, and I think you're right in that he was attracted to me, but only in a superficial sense. I was only fifteen, after all. Of course I used to lie in bed every night fantasising that he was as secretly crazy about me as I was about him. I used to write the most sentimental poetry about him—reams of it. I also used to read something deep and meaningful into even the smallest attention he gave me. Every glance my way was a searing, passion-filled gaze in my adolescent mind. Every conversation we shared had hidden love messages behind it.'

Angie gave a soft, sad laugh. 'The family had a habit of sitting out on the front veranda every night, looking up at the stars and talking. On a few occasions the others went off to bed, leaving Lance and me alone. You've no idea how that set my teenage heart a-beating. Only a fifteen-year-old fool would wind romantic dreams around idle chit-chat.'

'What did you talk about?'

'Nothing important. Just general stuff. Movies. Music. Books. Poetry. Looking back, I think Lance was only humouring me by claiming to find my tastes and opinions incredibly sensible and mature.'

'Maybe not, Angie,' her flatmate argued. 'You're a deep thinker, and maybe too sensible for your own good, I'm beginning to think. Far too sensitive, too. I can just picture you at fifteen. Very beautiful but very intense. Perhaps he didn't make a pass at you because that very intensity frightened him off.'

'Did I say he didn't make a pass at me? Yes, of course I did. Perfectly true, in fact. He didn't. He didn't have to. It was stupid me who made the pass. Eventually.'

Vanessa's head whipped round to stare over at her. 'You did? Good Lord! When? Where?'

'It was the night before he went back to Sydney. Out on the front veranda.'

'What on earth did you do? Do tell.'

CHAPTER THREE

Go TO bed, Angie willed desperately. Please go to bed. He's going home tomorrow. Don't you understand? I need to be alone with him!

Angie got the shock of her life when her mother immediately rose and announced her intention to retire for the night. When her father quickly followed, then Bud five minutes later, Angie thanked the Lord for His mercy. She swiftly moved from where she'd been perched up on the veranda railing to sit down next to Lance on the steps, her heart thudding at her boldness.

Lance was dressed in shorts and a singlet top, Angie in similar garb. The day had been hot and the night air was only just beginning to cool. Not that Angie felt cold. Sitting this close to Lance was a highly warming experience.

She stared down at her long brown legs, then over at his, tanned to a golden bronze by the long summer days. Her left thigh was barely an inch from his. If she moved it slightly, their skin would touch. She kept perfectly still, knowing her boldness did not extend that far.

'You don't get night skies like this down in Sydney,' he mused, sighing and leaning back a little, the movement making his thigh brush against hers.

Angie jerked her feet up on to a higher step, her knees pressed together to stop them from trembling. So much for her boldness! 'I ... I wouldn't know,' she said shakily.

'Your mum tells me you're going to come to Sydney to university when you finish school,' he said.

'I hope to. If Dad can afford it. Let's hope we don't have a drought or a flood during the next three years.'

Lance frowned, as though it would never have occurred to him that one's fortunes could depend on the weather. 'If that happens, I'll pay for you myself.'

'Oh, I couldn't let you do that!' she exclaimed, despite being thrilled that he had offered. 'The Browns always pay for themselves.'

Lance sighed. 'So I've gathered from Bud. Damn it all, Angie, you *must* come to Sydney.'

'Must I?' she croaked. Her eyes locked with his and her heart filled to overflowing. He feels the same as me, she thought dazedly. He just thinks I'm too young for him to say anything. This is his way of saying he'll wait for me.

'Not that I'm sure I'd like you going to Sydney Uni,' he muttered, but Angie wasn't really listening any more. She was drowning in his beautiful blue eyes, thinking how wonderful he was and that she wanted him to kiss her more than anything else in the world. She would just die if he went back to Sydney without kissing her.

'What course do you want to do?' he asked.

'What? Oh ... er ... an arts degree, majoring in psychology, if I get a high enough mark. If not, I'll do a degree in Social Welfare. I want to work with people, you see. I want to help solve some of the social problems of the world.'

'That's a tall order, Angie—solving the world's social problems. But I think it's fantastic that you want to try. So, tell me, what do you see as the world's main social problem?'

'That's a hard one. There are so many problems. Look, this is probably a simplistic approach but I think if people made their lives simpler they'd be happier. The Western world is moving too far away from the family unit and family values. I'd like to encourage people to be more serious about marriage and their commitment to raising children, to appreciate how much time it takes to do both well.'

'And do you want marriage and children for yourself? Or will you settle for a career?'

'I don't see why I can't have both. Of course, my career would always play second fiddle to my family. My husband and children would always come first with me.'

'Mmm, I see I'll have to keep a close eye on you when you get to Sydney, or some smart bastard will whisk you off to the altar before you can say lickety-split!'

'You ... you won't have to worry about that happening, Lance. There'll only ever be one man for me.' Having gone this far, she turned her head and stared him straight in the eye.

Those eyes flared briefly wide with surprise, before narrowing to an expression he'd never bestowed on her before. His darkened gaze moved slowly over her face, dropping at last to her softly parted lips then down to where her breasts were clearly outlined against the thin material of her top. Suddenly, she knew what it was like to be the target of a man's desire. A *man's*, not a boy's. She felt her body respond, everything all at once hot and tight and tingling. Her face flamed along with the rest of her.

'You're only fifteen,' he said abruptly, as though reminding himself.

'I won't be fifteen forever,' she returned breathlessly.

'True... But when you grow up, you might change your ideas about who and what you want.'

'No, I won't,' she said, her voice firming. 'Mum says I'm as stubborn as old Wally Robinson's bull. I'll feel the same way about you in three years as I feel now.'

She shook his head, obviously still troubled by the situation.

'Wait here,' she whispered, and, jumping up, raced inside to her bedroom, returning within no time.

'I wrote this the first week you came,' she said, and pressed the piece of paper into his hands.

He read the poem in dead silence before folding the page and putting it down on the step, shaking his head all the while. For a long moment Angie thought she'd made an utter fool of herself. But then he looked up at her and she knew . . . She just knew she'd been right. He *did* feel the same.

'Oh, Angie,' he said softly. 'Sweet . . . sweet Angie.' And he reached out to touch her face lightly.

His fingertips were like flicks of fire against her already heated cheek, at the same time igniting other flames throughout her body. The words fell out of her mouth—reckless, breathless words.

'Kiss me, Lance. Kiss me . . .'

'You can't stop there!' Vanessa wailed when Angie suddenly fell silent. By this time they'd reached the block of units in North Sydney where they lived, parked in the underground garage and were making their way up the internal staircase to their neat little second floor unit.

'What happened?' she persisted.

Once she recovered her composure, Angie smiled wryly at Vanessa's enthusiasm for her story. Underneath her hard-boiled exterior, she was a romantic—like most females.

'Nothing much. He kissed me, just once. It was quite brief, really.'

'It couldn't have been *that* brief if you still remember it. And if it's totally turned you off all other men ever since.'

'I didn't say I was totally turned off other men,' Angie explained. 'It's just that I've been waiting for their kisses to do for me what Lance's kiss did. I guess it's a matter of a standard of chemistry never being reached again.'

'So what was so special about the way this Lance kissed?'

'I don't think there was anything really special about his technique. I think it was the way the kiss made me feel that was so special.'

'And how did it make you feel?'

Angie stopped at their door, her heart squeezing tight again at the memory. She inserted the key in the lock but didn't turn it, her hand freezing as the words were wrenched from deep within her. 'Like the world had tipped on its axis,' she choked out. 'Like I'd died and gone to heaven...'

It was crazy, but even after all these years she could still remember the feel of his steely arms winding tight around her, the heady, intoxicating effect of his lips possessing hers, the blindingly electric shock that had charged along her veins when his tongue had momentarily dipped past her eagerly parted lips.

But it was what he'd said to her afterwards which had caused the lasting damage.

'I'll write,' he had said thickly, when he'd put her from him. 'And when you're old enough, we'll be together properly. I promise...'

Perhaps he'd almost meant it at the time. She could give him the benefit of the doubt after all these years. But that didn't change the inevitable outcome of his thoughtless arrogance in making a promise he must have suspected he would not keep, in condemning her to years of hopeless longing. In a way, that kiss had ruined her life.

'Wow, Angie! You really were in love with him, weren't you? So what became of him? Where is he now?'

Angie snapped back to reality, firmly pushing the still upsetting memories of Lance to the back of her mind. 'Happily married to a very rich, very beautiful woman,' she said with seeming calm. 'They live in Melbourne.'

'What did the poem say? Can you remember?'

Of course she could remember. Every heart-breaking, humiliating word.

'Not really,' she hedged. 'It was just a lot of sentimental twaddle, much better forgotten.' Which was true.

'I presume he didn't keep in contact after he left,' Vanessa said drily. 'No letters or anything.'

Angie threw her a cynical look as she turned the key and pushed open the door. 'Only a polite note to my parents, thanking them for having him to stay.'

'Bastard. There again, Angie, it was only to be expected. He was way out of your league.'

Five minutes later both girls were sitting at the small kitchen table, sipping a reviving cup of coffee. Angie was off in another world—worrying about Debbie—when Vanessa returned to the subject of Lance.

'Did you see him again after that summer?'

'Yes. A few times.'

'No kidding. Where? When?'

'The first time was a few months later at his and Bud's graduation ceremony. The whole family travelled down to Sydney to celebrate the occasion.'

'And?'

'He was polite to me, but distant. And of course there was this very sexy-looking redhead hanging off his arm all the time.'

'You must have been awfully upset.'

'Crushed. I'd still been making excuses for him in my mind, telling myself that he was like so many males when it came to writing letters. I thought once we saw each other again everything would be all right. He would see I was quickly growing up— having turned a whole sixteen by then. He would tell me he was still waiting for me.'

Angie's rueful smile hid a wealth of remembered misery. 'Silly me. But it was Bud who finally put the nail in the coffin of my one-sided love that day, when he told me that Lance had been voted Superstud of the Year at the party his faculty had held the previous night. Seems he'd had more girl-friends in the past three years than porcupines have prickles. The redhead was the latest—acquired at that very same party. Bud was already taking bets with his mates on how long she would last.'

'Hmm. Maybe you had a lucky escape, Angie— getting out with only being kissed. He could have screwed you and your life good and proper if he'd wanted to. You have to give him some credit for not taking advantage of your youthful hormones.'

'Yes, I did think of that. Eventually. I also be-lieved I'd finally forgiven and forgotten, or at least gotten over him...till I literally ran into him in Sydney one day during my second year at university. I had a mid-morning lecture and my train had been late. I dashed out of Wynard Station, and was racing along the street for a bus when I collided with this man. You can imagine my surprise when I realised who belonged to the strong hands which reached out to steady me. I think Lance was just as surprised.'

'My God!' he gasped. 'Angie...'

Angie tried not to stare at him. But he looked so handsome, dressed in dark trousers and a cream sports jacket. And so sophisticated. Only twenty-seven, but the university graduate was gone forever, replaced by the elegant man-about-town he had always promised to be.

She hated her tongue-tiedness; she hated the way she couldn't stop staring at him; she hated the way her heart was instantly yearning and hoping once more. She hadn't gotten over him at all. Not for a moment.

His blue gaze swept over her, taking in her typical student dress of jeans and T-shirt, a canvas backpack slung over one shoulder, battered trainers on her feet. 'I see you made it to uni,' he said. 'Did you get into the course you wanted?'

'Yes,' was all she could manage. She'd pictured such a chance encounter happening ever since coming to Sydney, had run over in her mind how she would act. So cool, so casually indifferent.

But there was nothing cool or casually indifferent in the way she was gobbling him up with her eyes. Or the way her heart was pounding behind her ribs. God, what a fool she was!

'You're looking well, Angie,' he said. 'I was sorry I couldn't make it to Bud's wedding last month. I've been overseas on business. And I'm sorry I can't stay and talk. I'm on my way to meet someone.'

'Oh, that's all right. I can't stay either. I'm late too. Look after yourself. Bye.' And she was off, almost running.

'Where are you staying?' he called after her.

Her heart leapt as she ground to a halt and turned around. Oh, God, he wasn't going to ask her out, was he? Please, God, let him ask me out, she prayed.

'I need to know your address so that I can send you an invitation,' he elaborated.

'Invitation?' she repeated weakly.

'For my wedding. I'm getting married in October.'

'Oh...' Did she look as stricken as she felt? She must have, for suddenly he looked awfully apologetic.

His obvious pity was the saving of her.

Somewhere she found a smile, a bright, breezy smile to hide her inner weeping. 'Fancy that! Married! Well, congratulations. Look, why don't you send the invitation to Bud's place? I keep changing my digs. Must go, Lance. See you on your big day!'

*   *   *

'Surely you didn't go!' Vanessa exclaimed in appalled tones, glaring at her over the table.

Angie shrugged her admission.

'Gees, girl, you're a glutton for punishment!'

'You can say that again. What Lance can do for a dinner suit is criminal.'

'Why on earth did you go?'

Angie expelled a weary sigh. 'Curiosity, I guess. I wanted to see the woman who'd snared him. Besides, the whole family had been invited, including Mum and Dad. I really couldn't get out of it without having to answer some darned awkward questions.'

'And?'

'Sheer perfection, the bride was. Like a Dresden doll and just as expensive. I hated her on sight and worshipped Lance all the more. It was the worst day of my life.'

'What about your family in all this? Didn't they notice anything? Didn't they see you'd broken your heart over this heartless Don Juan?'

'I'm sure Mum was beginning to wonder. And I think Bud had guessed some time back. Perhaps as far back as the night of his and Lance's graduation. He'd made such a point of letting me know about Lance's reputation where the opposite sex was concerned. Even at the wedding he said he'd make a fortune if he took bets on Lance's marriage lasting. He said Lance was a great guy but that he wasn't cut out for monogamy. He added, rather pointedly, I thought, that it wasn't always his fault.

That a lot of the times silly girls—this said looking straight at me—threw themselves at him.'

'Pretty lame excuse, if you ask me. Hard to rape a guy, I say. Did you speak to lover-boy himself at the wedding?'

'I tried not to, but Lance seemed to deliberately seek me out. Lord knows why. Maybe he was finally suffering from a guilty conscience. He gave me this ghastly kiss on the cheek, then told me rather stiffly that he hoped life would bring me everything I'd ever hoped for, that he thought I was the nicest girl he'd ever met and that he wished the world could be full of people like the Browns.'

'Oh, dear,' Vanessa sighed. 'Hardly the thing to say to turn you off him, was it?'

Angie swallowed the lump that had suddenly filled her throat. 'No,' she confessed. 'Not quite...'

Vanessa was frowning at her. 'You're not *still* in love with him, are you?'

'No, of course not,' she returned impatiently, standing up abruptly to carry her empty mug over to the sink. 'That was donkey's years ago. Don't be silly.'

Vanessa joined her at the sink. 'I hope you're telling the truth, for it *would* be silly of you to still be in love with him. It's also silly for you to keep knocking back other men because of the way some rich creep once made you *feel*. Get your head out of the clouds, Angie, and get real. You're not getting any younger, you know. One day you'll wake up and you won't see a cross between Elle

MacPherson and Sophia Loren in the mirror, and then it'll all be too late!'

Angie had to laugh. Vanessa had a turn of phrase which could be highly amusing. A cross between Elle MacPherson and Sophia Loren, indeed!

'You're going to your brother's birthday party tonight, aren't you?' Vanessa went on, with a devious gleam in her eye.

'Yes . . .'

'Is it a big party or just a small gathering?'

'Bud's parties are always huge.'

'What's your brother do for a crust?'

'Well, he did a business degree, majoring in computer studies and marketing. But he went into advertising and he's been surprisingly successful.'

'Then his party should be full of eminently suitable candidates, shouldn't it?'

'Candidates for what?'

'Your first lover.'

Angie was about to protest when she stopped herself, all those maudlin memories of Lance sparking an uncharacteristic surge of recklessness. Maybe Vanessa was right. Maybe even Debbie had been right this afternoon. Life was meant to be lived. To remain ignorant and inexperienced just because she was clinging to a crazy dream was indeed silly.

'At least go with an open mind,' Vanessa urged. 'Promise me that if a suitable candidate shows up, whom you're genuinely attracted to, you'll think about giving him a chance.'

'All right,' she said, suddenly making up her mind to do just that. 'I promise.'

'Now you're being sensible.'

Which was what Lance had said about her more than once that summer. How sensible she was.

Well, she was sick of sensible! Her resolve to follow Vanessa's suggestion deepened. She would find herself a real lover as opposed to a fantasy one. It was time. Yes, it was definitely time!

'I'm going to make sure I look smashing tonight,' she said through clenched teeth.

'Attagirl!' Vanessa crowed. 'Go for it, sweetheart. You only live once!'

Ten o'clock that evening found Angie regretting the trouble she had gone to over her appearance. She received enough male attention at parties at the best of times. Done up as she was tonight, and smothered in perfume, she seemed to have reduced potential candidates to panting pursuers, thereby ensuring her revulsion. She hated men who came on too strong, who delivered obvious lines then expected her to melt instantly at their feet. If one more intoxicated fool said 'your place or mine', she was going to scream.

There again, she supposed it was her own stupid fault if they all thought she was on the make. She should never have curled her long auburn hair and worn it provocatively over one shoulder. Or let Vanessa talk her into borrowing her outrageous gold and crystal earrings, which were five inches long and looked incredibly sexy.

On top of that, she hadn't been able to wear a bra under the petticoat-style party dress she'd bought specially for the occasion, and her naked nipples were patently obvious under the silky material. She should have bought the black one she'd first tried on, but the salesgirl had talked her into the green, saying it matched her eyes and complemented her auburn hair.

If she'd tried the dress on instead of just holding it up against her, she'd have known that the green didn't camouflage her body as well as the black. Angie began to worry that from the back she might look totally naked under the dress, despite wearing tights with built-in knickers.

Spotting a glassy-eyed chap making a beeline straight for her across Bud's crowded living-room, Angie whirled and made a dash for safety, gripping her glass of wine firmly in both hands lest she spill it all down her front. She found a temporary sanctuary in the kitchen, where Bud's wife, Loretta, was happily refilling serving dishes with all sorts of party snacks.

'Oh, hi, Angie. My, but you do look slinkily glamorous tonight. Bud said you had all his workmates drooling. Now I can see why. You had a jacket on when you first arrived, didn't you? Darn, there goes the front doorbell again. Could you get it for me, love?'

'Sure.' Angie didn't mind at all. It was better than going back into that room with all those heavy-breathing yuppies.

She sipped her wine as she made her way along the downstairs hall towards the front door, thinking as she went that Bud had really done very well for himself for a country boy from Wilga. A thriving career as an advertising executive, a lovely home in the leafy North Shore suburb of Turramurra, a very pretty wife and a delightful little boy, named Morris after their father. All this, and only thirty today. Remarkable.

Angie opened the door and promptly froze.

The man standing on the front porch, with his hands deep in his trouser pockets and an overnight bag at his feet, had his back to her. But she knew immediately who that well-shaped fair head belonged to. She'd have known him from any angle.

It was Lance.

CHAPTER FOUR

HE TURNED slowly at the sound of the door, moving with that lazy, indolent grace which she remembered oh, so well. There was no man who could mount a horse like Lance. There was no man who looked like him, either.

Even at thirty-one, Lance was still breathtakingly handsome. The lines around his eyes and mouth did not detract from the brilliance of those beautiful blue eyes, or the sensual appeal of that perfectly sculptured mouth. If anything, they added a very attractive maturity, which Angie preferred to his once almost pretty-boy look.

His body hadn't changed, though. Perhaps it would have been better if it had. A few pounds of flab to mar its male perfection might have provided some protection from the way it had always affected her.

How was it, she wondered caustically as her eyes travelled with an almost resigned fascination over him, that he could look so sexy in an ordinary pair of grey trousers and a simple white shirt?

A bitter taste invaded her mouth as she recalled the occasion of that unexpected meeting in Sydney, when she'd been flustered and tongue-tied. Angie vowed that this would not be a repeat performance, despite the way her heart was instantly racing.

Her green eyes stayed cool as they lifted to meet that brilliant blue gaze. 'Hello, Lance,' she said casually. 'Long time, no see.'

For a few seconds he didn't reply as he gave her as thorough a once-over as she had given him. It piqued Angie when his expression revealed a degree of surprise, plus something else that she couldn't quite identify.

'Yes, it is,' he said slowly. 'I see you've changed somewhat.'

'For the better, I hope,' came her almost challenging comment as she sneakily moved her glass to cover her left nipple, the one which her hair didn't reach.

His smile was wry. 'Hard to improve on perfection, Angie.'

He could not have said anything to annoy her more. For it was so insincere! She found a smile as wry as his. 'You always did know what to say to turn a girl's head, Lance. But, tell me, what are you doing here? Is Bud expecting you?'

'No.'

'You do realise it's his birthday today, don't you?' she said archly. 'And that we're having a party in his honour.'

'Yes, of course. That's why I came.'

She frowned down at the bag at his feet. 'You look like you're aiming to stay for longer than the party.'

'For a night or two. But only if Bud has room.
I can just as easily go to a nearby motel for the
night. I have my car.'

She frowned some more. 'Are you saying you
drove up from Melbourne just because it's Bud's
birthday?'

'Partly.'

'What does that mean?'

'It means, Angie, my sweet, that my wife and I
have agreed to a divorce and I felt the sudden need
to get away and see old friends again.'

Angie congratulated herself on taking this news
so nonchalantly. At least on the exterior. 'You've
left your wife?'

'Aah, now, I didn't say that. She left me,
actually.'

'Why?'

His casual air suddenly dropped, irritation
flaring. 'For pity's sake, Angie, must I stand here
answering questions? I've just driven all the way
from Melbourne. I'm stiff as a board and damned
tired. I need a shower and a drink. Your mother
wouldn't have left me languishing on the doorstep
like this. She would have given me a big hug and
bundled me inside, post-haste.'

'Indeed. Well, I'm not my mother, am I? And
I'm more into kissing than hugging. Would you like
to kiss me hello, Lance?' she taunted, thrilling to
the foolishnes of her words.

He stared at her. 'Are you drunk or something?'

'No.' But I'd like to be, came the
savage thought.

'Then why are you acting like this?'

'Like what?'

'So unlike yourself.'

She laughed. 'How would you know what I'm like these days? The only Angie you ever knew was just a kid—a silly, impressionable kid who once thought the sun shone out of you.'

'Well, it's perfectly clear you don't any more,' he muttered testily.

She could hardly believe her ears. He was actually sounding disappointed that her once obvious hero-worship of him had disappeared.

'Oh, do stop scowling, Lance, and come inside. I'll go get Bud for you.'

Bud was as amazed as she was.

'Good God. Lance? *Here*?'

'His wife's left him,' she whispered to her brother.

'Hmm. Doesn't take too many guesses to work out why. I always said Lance was never cut out for monogamy.'

'Apparently he drove all the way from Melbourne today because he wanted to celebrate your birthday with you. Says he also wants to stay the night.'

'Well, of course he can stay the night. He's my friend! Go tell Loretta we have an overnight visitor, will you, Angie?' And he raced off towards the front hall.

Loretta was back in the kitchen, this time loading the dishwasher. She took the news of Lance's unexpected arrival and anticipated stay as cheerfully as Angie's mother would have, giving Angie new insight into why she and Bud were so compatible.

'How nice for Bud. He hasn't seen Lance since his wedding.'

'Neither have I,' Angie said.

Something in her tone brought a sharp look from her sister-in-law. 'You're not still carrying a torch for him, are you?'

Angie blinked her surprise, and Loretta smiled softly. 'One would have had to be deaf, dumb and blind at that wedding not to know you were heart-broken that day. Bud told me later that he tried to make you see that Lance wasn't the right man for any girl, let alone his much-loved sister. Did he succeed?'

Angie shrugged. 'I'd be lying if I didn't admit I still find him awfully attractive. But I'm cured of anything more.'

'I hope so. Married men are always trouble.'

'He says he's getting a divorce.'

'That's as popular as the cheque's in the mail,' Loretta said drily.

'You don't have to worry about me, Loretta. I'm once bitten, twice shy where Lance Sterling is concerned.'

'I know Bud will be relieved to hear that.'

'I'll be relieved to hear what?' the man himself said as he came into the kitchen.

'That Angie's cured of Lance.'

Bud looked hard at his sister. 'She'll need to be, dressed as she is tonight.'

Angie bristled. 'Meaning?'

'Meaning Lance is not the sort of man to ignore the signals you've been giving out tonight, dear sister of mine. On top of that, he always did fancy you.'

'Come on, Bud, you're living in the past. And give me a break. I'm twenty-four years old now, not fifteen. I think I can handle myself where men are concerned—Lance included.'

Brave words, girlie, that voice mocked inside her head again. Want to put them to the test?

Her brother sighed. 'Yeah, you're right. I'm being paranoid. Lance seems to have changed too. He was very quiet just now—not at all like his old self. I think that marriage must have knocked the stuffing out of him.'

'Where did you put him?' Loretta asked.

'In the main guest-room. He's having a shower. I'm supposed to be mixing him a Scotch and dry and taking it up to him. Since you're so cured, Angie, you can do that. I really should get back to my other guests. You should, too, Loretta. You've been in this kitchen long enough.'

Panic claimed Angie immediately. She wanted to scream out that she wasn't that cured yet, but the idea of taking Lance up a drink while he was in the shower did have a certain perverse appeal. Who knew what she might accidentally see?

Memories of their swimming together in the creek at home came back in a rush. Lance had such a great body. A swimmer's body. Wide of shoulder, slender of hip, with long, tapering muscular legs. He'd been a champion swimmer at university, only missing out on the Olympics because he would never take training seriously.

That had always been a problem with Lance. He'd never taken anything really seriously. But that had been part of his attraction too. Serious-minded, deep-thinking Angie had been intrigued by someone who didn't seem to plan or worry about much.

Not that he had to. He'd been born clever and handsome and rich—the rich part being the most influential in forming Lance's attitude to life. Everything just fell into rich people's laps, it seemed. Everything had certainly fallen into Lance's lap—females included.

This last thought brought a sour grimace to Angie's face. She threw together a whisky and dry which would have made the heroine in *Raiders of the Lost Ark* finally slide under the table, and carried it upstairs, wondering what her motivation was in mixing such a stiff drink. Was she trying to anaesthetise Lance, or prime him for seduction later on?

She gasped with shock at this last thought, grinding to a halt on the top landing. But the shock quickly changed to defiance. Hadn't she promised Vanessa that if a suitable candidate showed up at the party tonight she would give him a chance to become her first lover? Who better than the man she'd wanted to be her first lover all along?

God, maybe she was drunk after all. How many glasses of wine had she had before Lance arrived? Two? Three? No, only two. She wasn't drunk, but she also wasn't acting like her usual sensible self either, as Lance had so accurately pointed out at the door. Suddenly she felt even more reckless than she had earlier, and just a little bit wild. Wild as in angry.

Oh, yes, she was angry. Angry at Lance. He had no right to show up here tonight and spoil everything for her again. It wasn't fair! He would have to pay. She would make him pay. With his body!

She didn't knock, just bowled straight on in. But as luck would have it, Lance was out of the shower and almost dressed. He still looked very inviting, with his shirt open to the waist, giving her a splendid view of his golden and gloriously hairless chest.

His eyes snapped up at her abrupt entry, glaring his disapproval at her as he finished buttoning his shirt and then his cuffs. 'I'm sure your mother taught you to knock before entering a gentleman's room,' he said sharply, tucking the shirt into the waistband of his trousers.

'I'm sure she did,' Angie countered. 'I'll remember that next time I enter one.'

He sucked in a startled breath, his blue eyes darkening. 'Are you trying to pick a fight with me for some reason, Angie?'

Yes, came the totally unexpected but brutally honest thought. For if I don't, I just might throw myself at your feet and tell you that I still love you—have done all these years!

Angie turned away before he could see the stricken look on her face. Oh, God. It couldn't be true. It *shouldn't* be true. But it was...

She whirled back, a plastic smile on her face. Her head was spinning and she had no idea what she was going to do now. Her idea from a moment before, of a crazy seduction, suddenly seemed even more appropriate—maybe even essential.

For the first time in her life Angie wanted Lance to be as heartless a womaniser as he'd always been painted. For she didn't have much time. There was no doubt that he would return to Melbourne in a day or two. She would never have another chance. Maybe all she had was tonight.

'That *was* bitchy of me, wasn't it?' she said, trying to bring a seductively soothing quality to her smile. 'I was only teasing. Here's your drink. Bud asked me to bring it up to you.' She handed it over, then perched on the edge of the bed, hitching her dress up over her knees as she saucily crossed her legs.

'So what happened to make your wife leave you?' she asked, still smiling. 'Have you been a naughty boy again, Lance?' One part of her wanted him to say he'd been a very naughty boy. Another part wanted him to deny adultery, to claim he'd done his best to make his marriage work but found it couldn't because he'd never really loved his wife. He'd really been in love with someone else, you see. A girl named Angie.

He stared at her legs while he swallowed a deep gulp of the drink, grimaced, then placed the glass down on the nearby dressing-table. Still saying nothing, he picked up a comb and started combing his hair in the dressing-table mirror—his lovely, thick, wet dark blond hair. Angie watched it fall into perfect place, hating every single obedient lock, wanting to clasp great clumps of it with cruel hands while she pulled his mouth down on to hers.

A deep shudder ran through her. She had never thought herself capable of such feelings, of such a savage passion. It made her afraid of what she might do afterwards, if she went to bed with Lance and it was as incredible as she expected that it might be.

Suddenly she became aware that he was staring at her in the mirror. Not at her legs, this time, but deep into her eyes. 'Why do you want to know about my marriage?' he asked.

Her shrug was marvellously indifferent. 'I'm just curious, that's all. Bud always said it wouldn't last.'

His eyebrows shot up as he turned around. 'Is that so? And did he say why?'

'I dare say he thought the man voted Superstud of the Year wasn't good husband material.'

Lance went awfully still before shaking his head slowly and sighing. 'Dear old Bud,' came his dry remark. 'And I thought he was my friend.'

Angie bristled at the implied criticism of her brother. 'Bud *is* your friend,' she snapped. 'His saying that didn't make it so, Lance. If your marriage failed, look to yourself.'

'Oh, I do, Angie. Indeed I do. I made a big mistake marrying Helen.'

'I hope you're not blaming her now.'

'I blame no one but myself.'

'So you're definitely getting a divorce, are you?'
Angie asked, hating herself for wanting to know so
desperately. What difference could it possibly make
to her, or her life? Lance was only up here for a
night or two, then he would go back to Melbourne
and his own world of high-fliers and other women
like Helen. 'There's no chance of a reconciliation?'
she added, in what she hoped was a carefree
fashion.

'None,' he grated out, sweeping the whisky glass
up for another gulp, followed by another pained
grimace. 'Hell, Angie, what did Bud put in this?
It's strong enough to kill a brown dog.'

'Don't blame Bud. I made it. I thought you
looked like you needed relaxing.'

'You could be right there. But not this way.' And
he placed the drink down. 'So, tell me, Angie, has
life brought you all you ever wanted? Is there some
eager young man waiting downstairs for you to
return to his loving arms?'

At that moment, Angie wished she'd put arsenic
in his drink. 'Actually no, Lance,' she returned with
a coldly brittle smile. 'I'm between boyfriends at
the moment. As for my other ambitions, I *am* only
twenty-four, and only three years out of my degree.
I need a little more time before I can change the
whole world. Though I realise now that some
things—and some people—can never be changed.'
This with a sour look at Lance.

'Look, drop the acid barbs, will you? It's Bud's
birthday, and if I remember Bud, there'll be music

and dancing downstairs. I could do with some music and dancing at this moment, believe me.'

Taking Angie's nearest hand, he pulled her somewhat abruptly to her feet. She stumbled slightly and his other arm shot out to steady her, then snaked slowly round her waist. Startled, her green eyes widened as they flew to his, only to meet a decidedly cynical gaze.

'Don't look so surprised, Angie,' he drawled. 'Isn't this the sort of behaviour you would expect from an unconscionable rake like myself? I'm just taking you up on that hello kiss you offered me earlier on.'

Panic-stricken, Angie turned her face away from his descending mouth. 'Too late,' she muttered through clenched teeth as his lips brushed her cheek. 'I only give hello kisses at the door, not in bedrooms.'

He cupped her chin and brutally forced her face frontwards. 'Then call this a goodbye kiss,' he ground out.

No, she tried to cry out, but his kiss obliterated the word before she could do more than open her lips.

The memory can certainly play tricks with your mind, Angie thought dazedly as Lance's lips took violent possession of hers. She'd told Vanessa that his kiss had made her think she'd died and gone to heaven. Either she'd been mistaken, or things had changed dramatically. There was nothing at all heavenly about the lips which were clamped to hers at that moment, prying them apart with so much force that her lips were ground back against her teeth. It was sheer hell.

But no sooner had Angie decided that she'd been mad to imagine she'd loved him all these years than everything changed. The fingers gripping her chin suddenly gentled, then trailed tantalisingly down her throat. Another hand slid up her back and into the hair around her neck. The vice-like lips lightened their gruelling pressure.

And then—then, when she was sighing with relief and almost relaxing into him—*then* his tongue moved slowly and incredibly seductively into her mouth.

It dipped deep, then withdrew, then darted back, coupling with her own tongue in an erotic dance which went on and on and on.

Angie was polarised with the most intense pleasure—eclipsing everything she had remembered. Sensations were racing to every corner of her body, every last nerve-ending, every tiny fibre of her being. She felt shattered, yet at the same time almost complete. This was where she'd always wanted to be—in Lance's arms, his mouth fused with hers, their bodies pressed together. Only by making love would she be totally complete.

In silent yearning she reached for that end, her hands instinctively lifting to splay into his hair, to keep his mouth on hers, to press herself closer and closer. She heard his groan of raw desire, felt it rising against her. Her own desire rose to meet his, and her hips moved with instinctive need.

'Auntie Angie...'

The small voice pierced the fog of her passion with crippling effect. She gasped away from Lance's mouth, the wild wonder of it all immediately replaced by sordid reality as Angie was faced with the knowledge that she had only been moments away from letting Lance do whatever he wanted with her.

'I want a dwink of water,' three-year-old Morris cried, when his auntie looked over Lance's shoulder at him.

With a soft moan of self-disgust, she pried herself out of Lance's seemingly frozen arms and turned to her nephew, who was standing just outside the open doorway—another factor in Angie's mortification. My God, she thought, anybody could have walked by and seen us. What if Bud had come up?

Her insides churning, she scooped up Morris and carried him swiftly down towards the main bathroom and his bedroom. 'Your mummy and daddy won't be too happy with your being out of bed, young man,' she said breathlessly. 'I won't tell them if you promise to drink up your water real quick, then go back to sleep.'

'Who was that man kissing you, Auntie Angie?' Morris asked with a child's innocent puzzlement.

'He's a friend of your father's and mine,' she told him, hoping that would be a satisfactory answer. Morris was going through an inquisitive stage when he asked questions about everything.

'Why was he kissing you? Are you going to marry him, Auntie Angie?'

Angie felt sick inside. 'No. I'm not going to marry him, Morris. We haven't seen each other for a long time. People kiss each other when they haven't seen each other for a long time.'

'Yes, but——'

'How much water do you want?' she broke in, hoping to distract the child. 'A whole glassful or only half a glass?'

Angie managed to get Morris back to bed without any more embarrassing questions. She only hoped he wouldn't relay the news in the morning, of his Auntie Angie kissing one of Daddy's friends in the guest-room. Briskly she tucked him in, pecked him on the forehead, and was about to escape when Morris decided that he couldn't possibly go to sleep without being read a story.

Sighing, Angie did the honours with *Toby, the Tonka Truck* which proved to be quite a long story. By the time she finished it, Morris was sound asleep. For a long moment she stared down at the sleeping child, with his olive skin and black curls, the unbidden thought coming that a son of Lance's would probably be as fair as Morris was dark. Asleep, he would look like a golden angel.

Her heart turned over and, closing her eyes, she bent to kiss Morris on the forehead, her mind still full of that imaginary golden angel. 'Love you,' she whispered softly.

With a sad sigh, she opened her eyes, closed the book, put it aside and stood up. After carefully snapping off the bedside light, she had turned to tiptoe out of the room when she encountered Lance, lounging in the doorway. Clearly he'd watched the whole proceedings; the thought disturbed and then infuriated Angie. When would she rid herself of these stupid futile dreams?

She shoved him out of the doorway none too gently, and quickly closed the door before he said anything and woke Morris.

'Smart little tyke,' Lance said. 'Trust Bud to have a great kid like that.'

Angie eyed him with a mixture of surprise and annoyance. 'Jealous, Lance?'

'Of course.'

'In that case, why haven't you had children of your own?' she snapped. 'Or have you been too busy with your jet-setting life to fit them in?'

'If you're going to answer your own questions, Angie, then why should I? I might ask you the same question. Why haven't you converted that obvious maternal instinct of yours into first-hand reality? Why haven't you found some nice man to marry by now and had a couple of kids?'

God, he had a hide to ask her that! The man had to be thick as a brick! 'No doubt I will,' she said, smothering her hurt behind a cold smile. 'Eventually. But for now I happen to have a career.'

'Ah, yes . . . your career. Bud tells me you're directing schoolgirls along the path of right and righteousness.'

'Trust someone like you to sneer,' she countered tartly. 'People with no morals and standards always mock those who have.'

His eyebrows shot upwards. 'Watch it, Angie. People in glass houses shouldn't throw stones, you know.'

'Meaning what?'

'Meaning ten minutes ago you showed a tendency to loose morals yourself. You could have knocked me over with a feather when I found you'd become one of those females willing to open their legs after one kiss.'

Her hand flashed across his cheek, the sound harsh and biting. 'Bastard,' she hissed, everything inside her trembling wildly.

His own hand lifted rather indolently to rub his reddened cheek. 'Was that for just now, Angie, my sweet? Or nine years ago?'

'Both,' she bit out.

His gaze narrowed on her, his brilliant and deceptively intelligent eyes darkening to a deep thoughtfulness. 'Good,' he said at last, in an oddly satisfied voice.

'What's good about it?'

'Not all that much, I guess. Come on,' he said, grabbing her hand and tugging her along the hall. 'Let's go downstairs and dance.'

Outrage had her wrenching her hand out of his and grinding to a halt. 'Just like that? You expect me to go downstairs and dance with you after you insulted me?'

His mouth broke into one of those old smiles of his, dazzling and totally disarming. 'Hell, Angie, *you've* been insulting *me* ever since I got here. What's a few insults among friends? Besides, I don't think what I said was an insult. I rather like females of easy virtue. Saves a chap a hell of a lot of lies.'

'Oh, you——' He shut her up with another kiss. A lightly teasing brush of lips which evoked a soft little moan of despair mixed with delight. 'You're wicked,' she whispered shakily.

'And you're gorgeous,' he drawled, his eyes narrowing sexily as he picked up one of the long curling strands of hair that covered her appallingly peaked nipple and drew it slowly between her lips.

A wild heat flooded those lips, and then her limbs. Weak with desire, she reached out to grip his shoulder, her lips falling apart as she unconsciously pulled him closer.

'Later, I think, sweet Angie,' he murmured, withdrawing the lock of hair and smoothing it down back over her breast, brushing over the pained peak as he did so. 'I have an aversion to starting anything I can't finish, and I have a feeling that brother of yours might shortly make an appearance.'

Angie's nostrils flared as she sucked in another indignant breath. 'And I have an aversion to men who make arrogant presumptions,' she flung back at him. 'I'm not as free and easy with my favours as you think, Lance.'

'No?'

'No.'

'How interesting...'

'Not really. You like your females easy, remember?'

'Usually. But for you, my sweet Angie, I'd be prepared to make an exception.'

'Stop calling me that!' she snapped. 'I'm not your sweet Angie any more. I'm not your Angie in any way, shape or form. I despise you, Lance, and all men like you. You wreak havoc wherever you go. You smile and you laugh and you dazzle, but you're all show and no substance. You come here tonight and try to seduce me within five minutes of landing, while your poor wife is probably crying her eyes out back in Melbourne.'

'I doubt that,' Lance snarled, all the dazzle gone from his face. 'I doubt that very much. Far from crying, Helen is probably at this very moment bonking her head off with her current lover.'

CHAPTER FIVE

For a second Angie was stunned, sympathy sweeping in for the angry man standing before her. Till the truth sank into her addled brain. Then sympathy turned to sarcasm. 'So she'd finally had enough, had she? Gave you back some of your own medicine.'

Lance simply stared at her. 'You're incredible, do you know that? You really think I'm a cross between Casanova and Bluebeard, don't you?'

'You can stop at Casanova,' she said drily. 'Murder is not your style. You're a lot of things, Lance, but violent is not one of them.'

'I wouldn't say that,' he muttered darkly. 'I can think of someone I'd like to strangle at this very moment.'

'Really?' she mocked. 'Yet only a moment ago you wanted to dance with me?'

His glare was savage, his eyes glittering dangerously. 'Who said I was talking about you?' he ground out. 'Let's go, lover.'

Any protest at this last tag was obliterated when Lance roughly repossessed her hand and hauled her downstairs. Neither did she object when he dragged her into a room where dance music was playing, and yanked her hard against him.

Their mutual anger lent a perverse edge to the unwanted desire that was still pulsating through Angie's veins. Soon, the throbbing beat of the music plus the heat of Lance's skin had her senses all awhirl, any common sense routed. Stupidly, she wound her arms up around his neck and sank against the body she'd always coveted, the body of the man she'd always loved.

But it was desire, not love, which was ruling her at that moment. It seemed to be ruling Lance as well.

Their eyes clashed—his hooded, hers widening. For she could feel his stark arousal pressing into her silk-covered stomach. Yet it was her own raw and highly primitive response to that arousal which surprised her the most. God, but she wanted him. And she wanted him *now*!

'Lance,' she breathed shakily.

'What?' he bit out, pulling back from her a little.

'I...I...'

'So here you are!' Bud broke in, his hand clamping on Lance's shoulder and spinning him away from a flushed Angie. Luckily the room was dimly lit, with disco-style lights flashing. That, plus the many other dancing couples, precluded Bud noticing too much. Thank heavens.

'I looked upstairs but couldn't find either of you,' Bud raved on heartily. 'For a second there, I thought you'd run off together.' Bud laughed, and so did Lance. Drily.

Privately Angie thought that her running off with Lance somewhere was a distinct possibility. Right now, she would do whatever he wanted.

It was a mortifying realisation, and one which brought her real personal pain. How could she possibly counsel other people on matters of life when her own could spin out of all control so quickly? She should have more will-power, more self-respect. Twenty-four years old and she was acting like an immature, hormone-filled teenager!

Angie would have been quite happy about being reduced to a state of mindless passion if Lance had cared about her.

But he didn't.

At best, he was physically attracted to her. At worst, he was using her as a way of getting back at his wife. Either way his desire for her was a very casual and fleeting thing, to be indulged in this one night and forgotten in the morning.

Angie, however, would not forget it in the morning. She could see herself now—torn by remorse and regret, plunged into despair and self-disgust. Lance would go off on his merry way, leaving her again to die another thousand deaths in the wake of his empty charm and superficial sex-appeal.

But, oh...how his charm could charm—and how his sex appeal appealed...

Even now, all she wanted was for Bud to get the hell out of here and let Lance take her in his arms once more.

Exasperation came to her rescue. If the man affects you physically like this, she lectured herself valiantly, then stay away from him, for goodness' sake. Don't look at him anymore. Don't dance with him. Don't go anywhere near him!

In fact, *go home*!

'If you'll excuse me,' she said swiftly, before she could change her mind. 'I . . . I have to go and see Loretta about something. You and Lance must have loads of things to talk about. I'll catch up with you later, Lance.'

Angie fled without looking back, surging past various gyrating couples and heading straight for the cupboard under the stairs where she'd put her jacket and bag.

Retrieving them both, she draped the black jacket over her shoulders, then closed the cupboard door and hurried towards the front door, opening her handbag as she went. It was a largish black patent leather number, with a zipper running along the top and one roomy cavernous area inside, filled to the brim with all sorts of female paraphernalia. Make-up. Tissues. Perfume. A nail file. Nail clippers. Bobby-pins. Safety pins. Comb. A mirror.

Plus her car keys.

Somewhere . . .

Angie ground to a halt, swearing under her breath as she blindly rifled through the mess with her hand. She encountered everything but her keys.

God, but that was so typical! Whenever one wanted to find something desperately, one never could. Speed was of the essence too. Any moment,

Loretta or Lance or Bud might appear, wondering what she was doing and where she was going. Her brother would be annoyed with her for leaving his party so early but she would survive his disapproval. She might not survive something else if she stayed.

'Lord, where are those damned keys!' she groaned aloud.

Frustrated, she raced over and tipped the entire contents out on to the hall console; the keys were the last thing to clatter on to the marble surface.

'Looking for this?'

Angie gasped when Lance materialised to reach over her shoulder and pick up the condom Vanessa had mischievously dropped into her bag and which lay with garish clarity among her make-up and other possessions.

Whirling, she went to snatch it back, but he was too quick for her, slipping it into his trouser pocket. Angie glared at him. No way was she going to try to retrieve it from there!

Her cheeks burning, she spun back to the console and scooped everything but the keys into her still open bag. Picking up the keys, she dangled them in the mirror on the wall for him to see. '*These* are what I was looking for. But do keep the condom, Lance. No doubt you'll be needing it before the night is out. A superstud like yourself won't have any problem finding some pretty little thing to oblige you.'

'Do you always carry condoms around with you?' he asked as she zipped up her bag and rammed it under her arm.

Angie turned to glare at him, livid at the look of hypocritical reproach on his face. 'Why not?' she flung at him, her defiant expression reminding her of Debbie that afternoon. 'A girl never knows when she's going to get lucky, after all.' Rather enjoying his ongoing air of shock, Angie lifted her chin proudly, then hurried down the hall and out through the front door.

The sight of a sleek black car parked behind hers in the driveway, barring her escape, brought a groan of dismay to her lips.

'Blast,' she muttered. 'Someone parked their damned car behind me.'

'I wouldn't think you should be driving anywhere,' Lance said quietly from behind her. 'You're obviously drunk.'

Now she really lost her temper. 'And why, exactly, must I be drunk?' she fumed, spinning round and planting furious hands on her hips. 'It wouldn't be because I've chosen to leave your not so salubrious company, would it? Or because I've decided to be the exception and not surrender to your oh, so irresistible charm this evening?'

'No,' he returned calmly. 'It's because I've finally realised you've been acting totally out of character ever since I arrived. Now, why would that be, I'm beginning to wonder?'

Her slow handclap reeked of sarcasm. 'Bravo, Lance. You've had virtually nothing to do with me for nine years and you claim to know what my usual character is. Believe it or not, old friend, a girl changes somewhat between fifteen and twenty-four. This is me these days, Lance,' she said, scooping off her covering jacket with one hand, clasping her bag in the other then twirling round so that he could see every inch of her provocative dress. 'It wouldn't be that you can't cope with your ''sweet Angie'' being sexually active, would it? Even nice girls *do*, Lance. And *I* do—quite often, in fact!'

The moment the lie was out she regretted it. Crazy as it was, she hated seeing the disappointment in Lance's face.

Or was it something else she glimpsed behind those suddenly clouded eyes of his? Maybe it was...defeat?

The idea of Lance feeling anything like defeat bewildered Angie. Yet his shoulders were beginning to sag and there was an air of wretchedness about his slightly slumped form.

Maybe, she conceded with great difficulty, maybe he was more upset about his marriage break-up than she'd believed. Maybe he'd really been in love with his wife...

As much as Angie hated *that* idea, it showed that Lance was capable of feeling deeply about a woman. Bud had had little to do with his friend since their marriages, so his old opinion of Lance's character might be totally out of date. Angie herself had just made the point that people changed. Well, maybe Lance had changed as well.

She'd no sooner starting thinking sympathetic thoughts about him than he snapped out of his dejected demeanour, straightening up and throwing her a ruefully sexy smile.

'You're right,' he said. 'I'm being somewhat of a hypocrite. You're only young once, and you're just as entitled to sow your wild oats as anyone else. Any reason why you can't sow some of them with me?'

Angie just shook her head. So much for Lance having changed.

'Nope?' he mocked. 'Oh, well, can't blame a guy for trying. Come for a drive with me, then?'

Angie stamped her foot in total exasperation. 'What is it with you? Can't you see I don't want to go anywhere with you? I just want to go home. If I knew who owned that damned car I'd get him to move it and——'

She broke off when Lance smiled a smug smile.

'It's *your* car, isn't it?' she said frustratedly.

'Sure is. Actually, Bud asked me to go buy some more beer from the local grog shop. He said you'd show me where to go. I'm sure he had no idea you were thinking of going home. Why are you, anyway? The night's still young. Who knows? You might get lucky, after all.'

Angie chose to ignore Lance's last remarks. 'Why doesn't Bud go get the beer himself?'

'Because he's finally cornered a very important potential client. You know what advertising people are like, Angie. Much the same as insurance salesmen. They're always working.'

Angie felt that underneath his light-hearted attitude Lance was denigrating her brother's profession. 'Well, at least Bud *works*,' she bit out.

Lance looked taken aback. 'You think I don't?'

Angie shrugged, aware that she'd been abominably rude to Lance tonight. Whether or not he deserved her contempt was not the point.

'One day,' he grated, taking her elbow, 'I'm going to sit you down and tell you some cold, hard facts about my life. You have a very jaundiced view of it. But not tonight,' he added as he shepherded her down the steep driveway past her small red Lancer and over to the passenger door of his car. 'Tonight is Bud's birthday party, some more beer is needed, and his sweet sister is going to show me where to get it!'

'I will, provided there's no funny business,' she stated firmly at the passenger door. 'No passes. No suggestive remarks. No nothing. Just down to the grog shop and back again. Then I get to take my car home.'

'Scout's honour,' Lance said, and crossed his heart.

'Hmph!' Angie grunted. 'I doubt you were ever a Boy Scout, Lance Sterling.' And she wrenched open the car door.

She didn't recognise the make and didn't much care. It was a rich man's car, which smelt of real leather and had probably cost a fortune. She climbed in and belted herself properly, determined not to make a single complimentary remark. Let him think that she often rode around in rich men's cars! Let him think whatever he damned well liked about her, as long as he kept his hands off!

'Second street on the right,' she told him sharply, once he'd reversed out and was heading in the right direction. 'There's a drive-in bottle shop a couple of hundred yards down on the left.'

There certainly was, but its driveway was crammed with cars. Lance parked in the street, growling, 'Be back in a minute,' before he alighted and strode off to get the beer.

Butterflies invaded her stomach as she waited for him to return. She wasn't sure why. Was it that she didn't trust Lance—or herself? Sitting there quietly in the car was certainly not conducive to sensible thinking. It allowed that devil's voice back into her mind, the one which told her not to let Lance get away a second time, to take what was on offer, even if it was only sex. After all, it wouldn't be just sex on her part, would it? It would be making love as well.

Yeah, right, she argued back silently. And what do you think would happen as soon as he found out you were a virgin? A man of his experience would know for sure. You wouldn't be able to pull the wool over *Lance's* eyes. Too bad you're not the free spirit you've been painting yourself to be all evening, then there wouldn't be any trouble.

What irony, Angie conceded bleakly. Who would have believed that her old-fashioned morality would cost her what she had always wanted most, besides Lance's love?

Still, her thoughts had calmed her agitation somewhat, and had made her see that to run off home like a frightened rabbit was totally unnecessary. Recalling her virginal state had strengthened her earlier resolve not to do anything with Lance. She would rather die than be on the end of his mockery!

He came striding back, smiling wryly over at her as he climbed into the car. 'You stayed,' he said somewhat drily. 'I thought you might run away again.'

'No,' she said. 'I'm done with running away for tonight.'

'And what, precisely, does that mean?' he demanded to know.

'It means, Lance, that I've decided not to go home after all.'

'You never did explain why you were leaving in the first place.'

'I guess I was worried you were lining me up as another notch on your gun.'

'Ah. Back to Casanova, are we?' He shook his head as he restarted the car. 'I can see I have no hope of changing your opinion of me. It's fixed in concrete in your mind. Still, maybe I can chip away at that concrete over time...'

Glancing over his right shoulder, he executed a perfect U-turn and accelerated back up the road, neither of them saying another word till he swung his car into Bud's driveway and braked barely an inch from Angie's bumper-bar.

'Very impressive,' she muttered caustically.

Lance laughed. 'Glad to see I've impressed you in some small way. There was a time, though, when I impressed you in just about every way, wasn't there? I could have said the world was flat and you would have believed me. I could have asked you to walk on water and you would have tried.'

Angie twisted to stare at him with pained eyes. 'That . . . that time is long gone,' she said, shaken by his words.

'True,' he bit out. 'But there *is* one way where I suspect I still make an impression. And that's this way,' he rasped, snapping off his seat belt and leaning over to capture her startled mouth with his before she could do a damned thing to stop him.

CHAPTER SIX

SHOCK held Angie compliant for a few seconds, giving Lance the opportunity to kiss her very thoroughly, and to very good effect. But, despite her pounding heart and swirling senses, Angie was just mustering her courage to bite his maurading tongue when it withdrew.

Unfortunately, Lance misinterpreted her moan of dismay.

'It's all right,' he whispered, raining soft wet kisses all over her face. 'I feel the same. This had to happen one day. You know it as well as I do.'

'No!' she gasped. Or was it groaned?

'Oh, yes,' he insisted, then kissed her again, as if to prove it. She did her best to ward him off, moving her head from side to side while her hands pushed at his shoulders, but both gestures proved futile.

'Don't be such a little hypocrite,' he muttered, grabbing her hands and pressing them into the leather seat on either side of her twisting head. 'You *want* me to make love to you. That's why you've been calling me names all night, because underneath you despise yourself for wanting me. That's why you tried to run away back there, because you were afraid to stay—afraid of what I might do.'

'I'm not afraid of you,' she spat at him.

'Then what is it you're afraid of?' he taunted. 'Surely not the consequences of our making love? Have you forgotten I've got your very own protection in my pocket?'

'I haven't forgotten a thing.'

'Which, of course, is the main thrust of your dilemma. I'm still being punished for what I did nine years ago. Would you believe me if I said I did what I did back then for you, sweet Angie? Would it be unthinkable to attribute me with some honour?'

'*Honour*?' she repeated in blank amazement.

'Well, maybe not honour,' he said drily. 'You always did produce dishonourable thoughts in me. But I tried to do the right thing in the end.'

Which just showed how much she had meant to him that summer. The only feelings she had inspired in him back then had been lust. Nothing more.

'And *now*, Lance?' she asked derisively. 'Are you trying to do the right thing now?'

'Hell, no, Angie. I can see this is my one and only chance to have what I've always wanted—in a fashion—and I aim to take that chance by fair means or foul.'

'Bud will throttle you if he comes out and sees us together like this,' she warned him.

'No one can see into this car. It has specially tinted glass. Besides, Bud isn't going to come out.'

'Wh—why not?'

'Because he's very, very busy with that potential client of his. On top of that, he has no idea we're out here.'

'But—but...'

'Bud didn't ask me to buy any beer. I made that up on the spur of the moment to get you alone.'

'Why, you...you... If you kiss me again,' she hissed, 'I'll bite your damned tongue off.'

'Thanks you for the warning, lover,' he murmured through a menacing smile. 'I'll make sure I keep away from those pearly white teeth of yours, in that case.'

His mouth landed at the base of her throat, and Angie drew in a sharp breath when he started to suck on the fluttering flesh he found there.

Bittersweet sensations warred with her pride and self-respect. God, but she did so want to give in. That devil's voice was back again, tempting her, tormenting her.

You love him. You want him. Let him.

Don't think about tomorrow. Don't think about being a virgin. Don't think about anything.

Lance put the issue beyond question when his mouth slid down from her throat to where her breasts were rising and falling on either side of the confines of the seat belt. Pushing back the left side of her jacket, he began to lick at the already hard nipple through her dress, wetting the silk till it moulded the rock-hard peak like a second skin.

At that point he started scraping his teeth back and forth across the exquisitely sensitised tip, stopping every now and then to moisten it again with his tongue.

Angie had to bite her own tongue to stop herself from crying out, so sharp were the sensations. An electric excitement charged along her veins, heating her blood and firing her brain. When he closed his lips round the nipple, her back arched as far away from the seat as the seat belt would allow, pressing her breast further into his mouth. He obliged by drawing the entire aureole within the heated cavern beyond his lips and suckling away like a greedy infant.

It blew Angie's mind.

'Oh, God, Lance,' she groaned.

He abruptly released her hands and they fell limply to her sides. His mouth stayed at her breast, even when both front seats suddenly sank from an upright position to a semi-reclining one. Angie found herself closing her eyes and sighing with surrender to whatever was going to happen. Nothing could stop her now, not even an earthquake or the eruption of a volcano.

She was the volcano, she decided dazedly. Feelings long dormant were being released, bubbling up within her, straining for release. She could feel the pressure-cooker tension behind the pleasure of the moment, feel the simmering heat which at any moment threatened to flare out of control.

He was back kissing her mouth, her eyelids, her ear, whispering erotic suggestions which sent small explosions of desire popping in her mind.

'Yes,' she whispered back blindly. 'Yes, please.' Only to wonder immediately what she'd agreed to, what she'd begged for.

She seemed to have the answer when his hands moved up under her skirt to begin peeling off her tights. She even lifted her buttocks to help him. Soon her shoes were gone and her tights were draped over the dashboard and she was naked under her dress. When his hands slid slowly back up her naked legs, taking her dress with them, she was beside herself with excitement. Any second now... Any second...

But he didn't touch her where she was dying for him to touch her; his hands lingered tantalisingly on her thighs, caressing her softly trembling skin, stroking the outside from hip to knee in long, teasing sweeps till she couldn't stand it any longer. Her legs moved restlessly apart, showing him what she wanted.

And he obliged.

Dear God, how he obliged!

Angie could not believe she was allowing him to do what he was doing. But, oh... the heaven of it all. Her breathing quickened. Her heartbeat soared. Everything in her seemed to be rushing upwards, yet inwards at the same time. She moaned under the spiral of wild pleasure, her hands finding his hair, twisting it in her fingers, till finally she wrenched his head up and away from her burning, bursting body.

'No!' she cried, not at all sure what she was saying no to, except that it was all too much—too intense, too frightening.

'It's all right,' he reassured her huskily. 'I was just about to stop. That's not what I want at all, either.'

Angie lay there, staring with wide eyes up at him while he struggled to manoeuvre himself to her side of the car and crouch between her legs. He didn't undress properly but he did protect them both, undoubtedly with what he'd pocketed earlier.

For a few moments he caressed her again, this time with knowing fingers, till she was arching away from the seat again in desperate need. Only the seat belt kept her from threshing wildly against that torturous touch, so that when he stopped, to lift her ankles up on to the outside edges of the seat and ease her bottom forward, she was beyond thinking of anything but having him inside her.

Yet the moment he began pressing against her virginal flesh, she tensed terribly. His sharp intake of breath brought more panic, his second attempt to penetrate making her muscles spasm even more tightly shut.

'God, Angie,' he ground out, probing harder. 'Relax, will you?'

'I . . . I can't,' she choked out. 'Oh, God . . . I just can't. I don't know how.'

'What do you mean, you don't know how?' he rasped, all pressure easing as he totally withdrew. 'Hell . . . are   you   saying   what   I   think you're saying?'

Angie wanted to die of humiliation and frustration. She hated herself and her inexperience at that moment. Hated everything and everyone. She groaned with the deepest chagrin, lifting her hands to cover her face.

Lance swore again. Then again.

Angie cringed inside at the sounds she heard. Clearly he'd decided not to continue. Clearly uptight virgins were not Lance's style.

'Dear God in heaven, Angie,' he finally rasped, unsnapping her seat belt, grabbing her hands and yanking her upright. The soles of her feet shot off the seat down on to the floor, her bare legs practically wrapping around Lance, who was still squatting in the space between the seat and the dashboard. Thankfully her skirt fell down over her lap as Lance snapped her further forward, their faces only inches apart.

'Why didn't you tell me earlier that you were still a virgin?' he interrogated harshly. 'Why did you let me believe you were some kind of good-time girl who'd have sex with anyone she fancied at any place, any old time?'

Angie shuddered under Lance's fury. She'd never seen him like this before.

'Hell, do you think I'd have treated you like this if I'd known?' he flung at her as a finale.

'T-Treated me like wh—what?' she stammered, confused by this last outburst.

He stared at her, then shook his head. 'I'm not sure if you're a total innocent, or more calculatingly wicked than any woman I've ever known. Which is it? *Are* you a professional tease? Do you get your kicks out of dressing up like this and seeing how many men you can have panting after you? Did you perhaps get out of your depth tonight,' he scorned, 'with a man who doesn't tolerate teases— a man you once *really* fancied?'

'No!' she denied fiercely. 'And yet, yes... in a way...'

'Which is it? Yes or no?'

'No, I'm not a tease,' she denied hotly. 'But, yes, I did dress up seductively tonight, and, yes, you're right—I do fancy you. I always did.'

'No kidding! Well, the dressing up seductively part wasn't for me, though, was it? You had no idea I'd even be here. So what was on your agenda tonight which called for this vamp image?'

Angie grimaced, then shook her head.

'Either you tell me, or I'll ask Bud,' he threatened.

'Bud doesn't know.'

'Doesn't know what? That you're still a virgin? Or that you're some kind of sick man-hater?'

'I am *not* a man-hater!'

'Then tell me the truth!'

'I... I decided today that I was f-fed up with being inexperienced,' she confessed, blushing and stammering. 'I... I thought it was well past time that I lost my virginity. I knew there'd be a lot of potential partners here at Bud's party tonight so I dolled myself up and... Well, I just... I just...'

She shrugged, hoping she'd said enough to satisfy his curiosity.

'You just what?'

His persistence began to annoy her. What was it to him anyway? He didn't really care about her. He'd simply shown up out of the blue tonight at a highly opportune moment then tried to take ruthless advantage of it, even if he didn't know it.

'Oh, do shut up, Lance. I'm sure even Blind Freddie could get the picture. You turned up just when I was ripe and ready to take a lover, and for a short while tonight I thought it might as well be you, since you had been my first love, after all. By the time I decided not to boost your insufferable ego any further, you'd rather spoiled me for any other man here this evening. You have a habit of doing that in my life, Lance,' she bit out. 'Spoiling me for other men. One of the reasons I'm still a stupid damned virgin is because of you!'

She scowled at him but he didn't scowl back. All the anger seemed to melt from his face as a tender expression took over. 'I don't think there's anything stupid at all about being a virgin in this day and age,' he said softly. 'But since I've spoilt you for any other man so far, then the least I can do is undo the damage I've done.'

'What . . . what do you mean?'

'I mean, Angie, my sweet,' he said, kissing her lightly on the lips, 'that you're quite right. It *is* high time you lost your virginity, but I also think your first experience should be with someone you really fancy, not some bloke you've picked up at a party. There's nothing special about a one-night stand. Therefore I'm volunteering to be your first lover.'

'But I thought . . . I mean——'

'Don't think, Angie,' he cut in with a strangely gentle firmness. 'Just do as I say and everything'll be fine. Firstly, tonight is not the right time, and this car is certainly not the right place for such an important occasion in your life. We'll put all this

fantastic bottled up passion of yours on hold for
another twenty-four hours,' he murmured, encirc-
ling her mouth with a fingertip till her lips gasped
apart and a shudder of delight rippled through her.

'God, but it's going to be good, Angie,' he
promised huskily, taking his finger away to kiss her
again.

'But I thought you'd be going back to Melbourne
tomorrow,' she protested weakly, everything already
going crazy in her head.

'No. I was never going to do that. As for now . . .
I'm going to get out of this car, if I can. You'd
better put your tights and shoes back on before you
do, though. And do up your jacket. I've pretty well
ruined that dress, I'm afraid. But no worries. I'll
buy you another tomorrow.'

Angie sat there in a stunned state while he
climbed over her out of the car. He groaned as he
straightened, probably because of the muscle strain
of being squashed up on his haunches for so long.
Finally, as though mesmerised, Angie did as he
suggested, pulling her tights back on and buttoning
up her jacket so the undoubtedly ruined dress would
not show. She was dimly conscious that underneath her clothes her body was still aroused, her
nipples still distended, the area between her thighs
acutely aware of the snugly fitting underwear.

But her still being turned on physically took
second place behind the emotion which welled up
within her soul when Lance leant into the car and
took her hand in his. His tender smile sent tentacles
of warmth curling round her heart, evoking all

those old feelings which had besieged her that long-ago summer—feelings which had nothing to do with lust. When he drew her from the car and upwards, everything around him went out of focus. Her eyes locked on to his and nothing else existed for her but Lance—his face, his eyes, and the love she imagined she saw in their brilliant blue depths.

It was his mouth crashing back down on to hers which snapped her back to reality. For Lance didn't love women. He only made love to them.

Oddly enough, this renewal of her knowledge of Lance's character no longer had the power to turn Angie off. She'd gone beyond that now. Once back in his arms, she was too weak to fight his incredible appeal.

She did what he told her to do. She stopped thinking. Her arms wound around his waist then up his back. Her tongue darted forward to move past his and into his mouth, sending wild tremors of pleasure down her spine.

It was Lance who drew back first, his face actually flushed, his breathing ragged. 'Hell, Angie, we have to stop this, or I'll never last the distance.'

'*We*, Lance?' she teased softly, while trying to get her own rampant desire under control. '*You* kissed *me*, remember?'

'Yeah, but did you have to be so co-operative?'

'Yes.'

Their eyes clashed, Lance shaking his head then smiling with rueful acceptance of her honesty. 'You always were a one-off experience, Angie. Come on, let's get inside before someone realises we're missing.'

'What time is it?' she asked as they made their way together up the driveway.

'Eleven-thirty.'

Angie ground to a halt. 'Is that all?' She recalled seeing the time on a wall clock when she'd been arguing with Lance in the hall. It had been ten to eleven.

They'd only been gone from the house forty minutes.

It felt like an eternity.

CHAPTER SEVEN

LANCE was right. Bud didn't even notice that they'd been absent. He was too busy being the life of the party, telling jokes and generally having a wow of a time.

Loretta, Angie wasn't so sure about—her sister-in-law having given her and Lance a suspicious stare as they wandered into the main party room together. She seemed to make a point of excusing herself from the group of people she was chatting to and coming over.

'I've been wondering where you two disappeared to,' she said. 'Been catching up on old times, have you?'

'Not exactly,' Lance replied smoothly, before Angie could think of a suitable excuse. 'I had Angie show me where to buy Bud some beer for his birthday. I came without a present, you see. Speaking of presents, what did you give Bud, Angie? I seem to recall your family had a rule in the old days that presents could not exceed thirty dollars. It was to be the thought that counted. Does that still apply?'

'It certainly does,' Loretta jumped in, seemingly relieved by Lance's answers. Apparently she agreed with Bud's view that Angie should share nothing but friendship with a man like Lance.

Too bad, Angie thought with a sudden fierce resolve. Lance was going to become her lover and to hell with what everyone else thought. Maybe it would only last for a night, or a weekend, or a week. But that short time with him would mean more to her than a lifetime with any other man.

Lance might be a compulsive womaniser but he had other qualities besides his sex-appeal to be treasured. There was a core of tenderness in Lance which was as captivating as it was rare. A sensitivity and sense of compassion which she had once appreciated, and which she was sure still lived within his soul.

Oh, yes, he was still easily moved to lust by a good-looking female—herself included—but just lust would have taken her virginity back there in his car. It would not have backed off, or begun planning something special for her initiation into sex. It would have ploughed on selfishly, and to hell with her discomfort or pain.

Lance might not love her, but he cared about her. Angie sensed that caring now more than ever and hugged the secret knowledge to her heart.

'So what did you buy him?' Lance asked, and Angie smiled mischievously.

'Something very useful.'

'What?'

'A pair of glow-in-the-dark boxer shorts. They have an arrow pointing to the appropriate spot.'

Loretta dissolved into giggles. 'I always did have to draw your brother a map,' she said, and Angie almost choked with laughter. Lance was chuckling too when the man himself joined the group.

'Must be a good joke if Loretta is laughing at it.' He smiled broadly as he put an arm around his wife's quaking shoulders. 'I love her dearly but her sense of humour leaves a lot to be desired sometimes.'

'Angie was telling us about her birthday gift to you,' Lance confessed with a wry grin. 'Loretta was saying she's always needed to draw you a map.'

Bud's smile seemed to freeze on his face. He recovered quickly, but Angie thought she detected an acid note in his reply. 'Well, no one could say the same about you, mate. You'd find your way around a woman's body blindfold.'

An awkward silence descended on the group for a few embarrassing seconds, till Lance laughed. 'Blindfold, eh? Now, there's a thought. Though, personally, I like to keep my eyes open when I make love.' And his eyes moved slowly to Angie's.

'Make *love*?' Bud scoffed. 'That's not what you used to call it, old chum. Still, I suppose it *is* a four-letter word. Hasn't quite got the same colourful flair, though, has it? Neither does it truly reflect your superstud status.'

To give Lance credit, he didn't react. He merely smiled with seeming indulgence and dry amusement at his friend. Angie had to admire his forbearance. Another man might have flattened him.

Loretta, perhaps sensing that the atmosphere was becoming strained, decided it was time to produce Bud's birthday cake. It was a welcome distraction for Angie, who felt so angry with Bud that she had a job giving him a birthday kiss after the singing and candle-blowing was over.

It wasn't like him to be so rude, and she couldn't understand his motivation. It wasn't as though he suspected anything between herself and Lance. Loretta's earlier suspicions seemed to have been doused as well, especially as Lance had moved off and started chatting up a tall, voluptuous blonde, who could hardly contain her delight at his attention.

Angie wasn't at all delighted. Jealousy stabbed deep into her heart. Jealousy, plus insecurity and a general feeling of inadequacy. Maybe even now Lance was deciding he would be a fool to have anything to do with a naïve and totally inexperienced virgin. He would probably prefer to spend his break in Sydney with someone who could cater to his undoubtedly sophisticated tastes in bed. The more Angie watched him with that woman, the more she was convinced any attraction she held for him was already on the wane.

When the blonde lightly touched Lance on his arm, then laughed up at him, her fears increased. There was something incredibly intimate about that laugh. And something incredibly sexy. Were they making plans for a secret assignation—maybe even later tonight? Angie could practically see them now, laughing in a motel bed together, their naked bodies entwined, the blonde's long legs wrapping around Lance as he bent his head to her very large breasts.

Angie choked down the bile which rose in her throat and launched herself across the room towards him. Lance seemed startled when she grabbed his arm and said she wanted to go home and needed him to move his car.

Quickly recovering, he excused himself from the blonde, who didn't look so pleased now.

'And where are you two off to?' Bud pounced as they made their way together towards the front door.

'Angie wants to go home,' Lance explained patiently, 'and my car's parked behind hers.'

Bud's obvious relief reminded Angie of how disapproving her brother would be of her becoming sexually involved with Lance. Not that she intended telling him.

Still, maybe that would never happen, now that Blondie had come on the scene. Angie's insides began to churn. She wished Bud would just disappear, so she could get Lance alone to tackle him on the subject.

'Goodnight, then, love,' Bud said, giving her a kiss on the cheek. 'Thanks for coming. I'm not sure I should thank you for that rude birthday present, though. Just wait till your next birthday comes along. I'll find you something that will make you go as red as a beetroot!'

Angie laughed. 'I'll look forward to it. Say goodnight to Loretta for me, will you, Bud? I really must go home. I have this awful headache coming on.'

'Do you really have a headache?' Lance asked her after he'd moved his car and returned to where she was standing by her own.

'Yes,' she snapped. 'And it has blonde hair and big boobs!'

'Ah...' He grinned at her. 'You're jealous.'

'And if I am?'

'If you are, sweet Angie,' he said, drawing her into his arms, 'then that's good. That's very good.'

'You wouldn't think it was so good if you were on the other end. There again, I suppose you're never jealous, are you?'

'I could be...'

'You're not going to sleep with that woman tonight, are you, Lance?' she asked, true anxiety in her face and words.

Lance lurched backwards as though she'd struck him, his arms dropping away, his eyes suddenly stormy. 'Damn and blast, but I'm getting fed up with this! What is it with you? Do you think I have such little control that I can't go one night without sex? I'm not some randy ram who ruts around indiscriminately. I do have *some* standards. Believe it or not, I like to know and respect a woman before I go to bed with her. I haven't had a mindless one-night stand since the night of my uni graduation party.'

'Oh! I...I'm sorry, Lance,' she apologised, confused by his heated defence of his own character. And not altogether convinced he was telling the truth.

'And so you should be,' he ground out. 'I've had about as much second-hand insult from the Browns tonight as I can take. It's got to stop, Angie. I'm not what you think I am. Hell, don't you have any respect for me at all? Have you agreed to have an affair with me only for the sex?'

Angie's confusion changed into total fluster. She dithered and hesitated and blushed till he solved the problem for her.

Lance stared at her. 'Hell, it *is* just the sex, isn't it?'

'No, of course not,' she denied through her fluster. 'I . . . I like you a lot. I've always liked you. You know that, Lance.'

'You *loved* me, Angie. That's a lot more than just like.'

'I *thought* I loved you,' she countered. 'I was only a child, for pity's sake.'

'You were more an adult woman at fifteen than my wife was at twenty-four!'

Angie gasped and stared up at him. He reached out and cradled her cheeks, drawing her gently up on tiptoe till their mouths met. 'You *loved* me,' he whispered into her softly parted lips. 'Don't deny it.'

A sob of admission fluttered from deep within her throat.

'Maybe you still do?' he suggested huskily.

She gasped again and drew back, green eyes wide and heart pounding. 'No,' she choked out, a wild panic claiming her.

'No?' he repeated, blue eyes narrowing on her.

'No, I don't still love you,' she stated, with a firmness which belied her inner upheaval. 'As you just said, I don't even know you any more.'

'Then you will,' he vowed somewhat darkly. 'Starting tomorrow.'

'Only biblically speaking.'

Frustration flared in his face. 'If you think that, then you don't know anything about really making love.'

'I don't pretend to,' she said sharply.

'Then don't pretend to know what will transpire between us tomorrow. Now, go home, Angie. I've run out of patience for this kind of conversation tonight. I'll pick you up tomorrow morning at eleven.'

'Eleven!'

'Yes, eleven.'

'Why so early?'

'Have you anything else you have to be doing tomorrow?'

'No...'

'Then be ready at eleven.' He went to spin away when she called him back. 'What?' he snapped.

'You... you don't have my address.'

'I'll get it from Bud.'

Angie grimaced. 'But I...I don't want Bud to know...'

His glare made her feel vaguely ashamed. 'I see,' he said rather coldly. 'Very well, tell me your address. Believe me when I assure you I won't forget it.'

She told him and he was immediately striding away from her, not looking back, his body language showing extreme annoyance. He'd obviously taken her last request as another insult—this suspicion confirmed by his banging the front door shut behind him.

Angie groaned her dismay out loud. She would have liked nothing better than to tell the world Lance was going to become her lover. *If* he loved her. If there was some guarantee that tomorrow night would be the beginning of a real relationship, not just a sexual rendezvous.

But Angie was not about to fool herself. Lance's claims didn't change the fact that his record with the opposite sex was hardly enviable. Maybe he had stopped having one-night stands after leaving university. But that didn't mean he hadn't had a huge turnover of girlfriends. His marriage failing after four years was hardly a recommendation for relationship-forming, either.

His promiscuity over the years probably wasn't all his fault, she conceded. His inherited wealth, plus the many talents God had given him, made him a compulsive target for women. Clearly they threw themselves at his feet all the time. Still, she doubted he'd been a faithful husband. She doubted a lot of what Lance had said to her.

Sighing, Angie turned and climbed into her car. Time to go home. Time to try to get some sleep.

Tomorrow was not many hours away. It was, in fact, she realised as she glanced at the clock on the dashboard, already here.

* * *

'You're pulling my leg!' Vanessa exclaimed.

It was five past nine and both girls had struggled out of bed shortly before, then padded out to the kitchen in pyjamas and slippers for some reviving coffee. While the kettle came slowly to a boil Angie had told her flatmate about the night before. And Lance.

'I'm beginning to wish I was,' Angie said, a rush of sick nerves claiming her stomach. 'I'm never going to be able to eat any breakfast, the way I'm beginning to feel.'

'Now, let me get this straight,' Vanessa resumed, once they'd settled at the kitchen table with their coffee. 'Lover-boy Lance has left his wife and——'

'His wife left him,' Angie corrected.

'Do you know why?'

'There's another man, I gather. From what Lance said, there'd been more than one.'

'You're telling me that Mr Irresistible's wife has been having affairs?' Vanessa said sceptically. 'After only four years?'

Angie shrugged. 'Maybe she was a slut.'

'And maybe her superstud husband was so busy servicing every attractive female he came across, he didn't have time for the little wife back home.'

'He says he's not like that any more.'

'For heaven's sake, Angie, he had you flat on your back within an hour or two of meeting you again. That's pretty good going, don't you think? And hardly the action of a recently faithful husband.'

'It might very well be the action of a recently faithful husband,' Angie argued, her face flushing with indignation as Vanessa voiced her own fears out loud. The cold light of morning rather made one see things differently. 'If he was completely conscienceless, he wouldn't have stopped once he found out I was a virgin.'

Vanessa gave her a pitying look. 'You don't believe that any more than I do. He's merely exchanged a few seconds of passing pleasure for a whole night's worth of proper bonking. He gave you a line of bull, darling, and you fell for it.'

Angie put her mug down with a clank. 'Hey! *You* were one who said I should get myself laid, remember? Well, I'm going to. Tonight. And Lance is going to do the honours.'

Vanessa gave her another pitying look. 'You still love him, don't you? It's the only explanation for your putting yourself through this torture.'

'What torture? Lance makes love like a dream. I ought to know. I had an advance sample last night in his car.'

'He might make love like a dream but the afterwards will be a nightmare! Hell, Angie, you pined over one bloody kiss for nine years. Lord knows what one entire night's expert lovemaking will do to you! On a scale of one for a kiss and ten for the real thing, you'll be a cot-case for ninety years!'

Tears suddenly flooded Angie eyes. 'You think I don't know that?' she choked out, jumping to her feet and running for the bedroom. She was already sobbing uncontrollably by the time she hit the unmade bed, face-down.

Vanessa wasn't far behind. 'Oh, dear,' she sighed, sitting down on the side of the bed and putting a sympathetic hand on her weeping friend's shoulder. 'You really should stop all that bawling. It's going to make your eyes red and puffy. Cinderella can be covered in chimney dust when Prince Charming arrives, but her eyes are never red and puffy. Look, don't take any notice of me. I'm probably just jealous. You go and bonk your brains out with him. Who knows? It might get him out of your system. Even if it doesn't, it might get *you* into *his*. Maybe, when the night is over, he won't want it to be over. Do you get my drift?'

Angie rolled over, blinking as rapidly as her heart was suddenly beating. 'Do you really think that's possible, Vanessa?'

'Hell, honey, if I were a guy and you presented yourself to me on a silver platter, I reckon I'd want to keep you on that silver platter for more than one miserable night. You're the genuine article, and genuine articles don't come along very often these days.'

Angie sat up and threw her arms around a startled Vanessa, hugging her fiercely. 'Oh, thank you for saying that!' she exclaimed excitedly. 'Thank you, thank you, thank you.'

'Lordie, Miss Claudie!' Vanessa said, extracting herself from Angie's fierce embrace. 'You are an emotional little thing under that cool exterior of yours, aren't you?'

Angie smiled as she dashed away her tears. 'Our family's rather given to hugging, that's all.'

'Does dear Lance know what he's getting to-night?' Vanessa asked drily.

Her question bewildered Angie. 'What do you mean?'

'Never mind,' Vanessa muttered. 'What are you going to wear for this momentous occasion?'

'I have no idea. Lance is picking me up at eleven.'

'Eleven!' Vanessa wrinkled her nose. 'Oh, yuk. There's nothing worse than doing it in the daytime. Takes all the romance out of it.'

Angie laughed. 'You are funny! But I don't think that's what Lance's plan is. He has some idea about my getting to know the new him first.'

Vanessa's eyebrows shot up. 'Really? That sounds promising.'

'I thought so too... at the time...'

'And now?'

'Now I just feel sick.'

'You can always back out. Ring him and say you've changed your mind.'

Angie shook her head vigorously from side to side. 'I could never live with myself if I did that.'

'Will you be able to live with yourself if this comes to nothing more than that kiss did all those years ago?'

'I'll have to, because there's no going back, Vanessa. And no changing my mind. I'll survive losing Lance again. I won't survive not doing this.'

'I suppose the experience will add perspective to your counselling abilities,' her flatmate said drily.

'My mother always said one should look for the plusses in every negative.'

'I doubt many women would rate sleeping with Lance a negative,' came Angie's equally dry retort.

'Really? I must get a gander at this god-like creature when he arrives to pick you up. Do let me answer the door.'

'Be my guest. My knees will be knocking by then.'

'Oh, no, they won't be. You'll sail out of here looking and acting as cool as a cucumber, because that's the way you are. Or at least seem to be on the surface.' A devilish gleam glittered in Vanessa's dark brown eyes. 'I'd sure love to be a fly on the wall later on when lover-boy takes you to bed. If he thinks he's getting a shy, quiet little virgin then he might be in for a shock or two. I suspect there might be a hot little number somewhere behind those prissy clothes you wear to school.'

'I wasn't exactly dressed prissily last night,' Angie reminded her friend.

'No, and look where it got you. Almost being raped in the front seat of a car!'

'I wasn't nearly raped at all. I was all for it till the last moment.'

'Which reminds me. Have a couple of glasses of champers or something equivalent before the real thing tonight. Relaxation is the name of the game, girl.'

'All right. I'll do that.'

'And I'll pop a few you-know-whats in your handbag in case Casanova has a memory lapse.

Nothing kills passion more quickly than having to dash out to the chemist at the last moment.'

'Yes, Teacher.'

'Don't knock it, honey. I wish I'd had an understanding flatmate to give me all this good advice before I did it for the first time. There again——' she stopped to flash Angie a wicked grin '——I didn't have a flatmate at fourteen.'

'Fourteen!'

Vanessa shrugged. 'I always was a precocious child. Now, shouldn't you be hot-footing it into the shower? Time and tide waits for no man. Neither does man wait for woman.'

Angie was still smiling when she closed the bathroom door. But as she stripped off her pyjamas and saw her naked reflection in the vanity mirror, her smile faded.

A nice body wouldn't be enough to capture Lance's heart. He'd had enough nice bodies to last a lifetime. And proving to be a hot little number wouldn't impress, either. No doubt he'd had some women who had been so hot they'd melted their satin sheets.

No, there was no point in Angie doing herself up sexily today. Or in trying to outdo all his other lovers in bed. She wouldn't be able to, anyway. It would be like trying to win an Olympic medal at a sport she'd only just taken up the week before the games.

But she could give Lance what perhaps he'd never had before. A truly loving experience. A night full of warmth and affection and genuine gratitude. For she was indeed grateful to him. No matter what his motive, he was about fulfil part of her deepest dream—the one she'd once expressed in the poem she'd given him nine years ago.

Angie still hugged that secret dream to her heart, and tonight—tonight, a small part of that dream would come true.

CHAPTER EIGHT

ANGIE'S flat was on the second and top floor of a rather old building in North Sydney, in a handy street tucked away behind the main business district. It was not far from the station, but unfortunately without any view of the nearby harbour or bridge.

The block had twelve flats in all, four on each floor. Angie's was number eleven. Its living-room window overlooked the street below, which proved to be an asset if one wanted to spy on people arriving or leaving.

At five to eleven Vanessa took up her position behind the half-closed venetian blind.

'What kind of car does he drive?' she called out to Angie, who was still in the bathroom, deciding if she should wear her hair up or down.

'Black,' came back the answer.

'Yes, but what kind?'

'I have no idea. It's not a sports car, but it's sleek and foreign-looking.'

'With roomy bucket seats in the front,' Vanessa added drily.

'And tinted windows.'

'It's just pulled up outside.'

'It *has*?' Angie squawked, dashing out of the bathroom, holding her hair on top of her head.

Vanessa looked her up and down. 'I just hate people who can wear any old thing and still look fantastic.'

'This dress is not any old thing!' Angie protested. Made of a bright orange linen, it was halter-necked and very fitted, hugging her figure down to just above her knee. 'It cost two hundred dollars new.'

Admittedly, she had bought it a couple of years ago, and worn it to death. But it always made her feel good, and was the least prim and proper thing she owned, other than the green silk party number she'd worn the previous night. Angie was only human, and had decided in the end that she wanted to look sexy for Lance.

'Should I wear my hair up or down?' she asked in desperation.

'Up. With little wispy bits hanging around your face and neck. Not too tidy or tight, either. Loose is sexy. And earrings are a must. I've got just the thing. Oo-ee. Lover-boy just got out of the car—which is an Audi, by the way—and you're right. He's scrumptious!'

'What's he wearing?'

'A bluey grey suit. Wow, Angie, I've got the hots for him already.'

'Hands off, Vanessa. He's mine.'

Vanessa laughed. 'Do you honestly think he'd look twice at me with you in the same universe? I'll just go get those earrings—and those other things I promised. You whack some pins in your hair. Then when lover-boy arrives don't come out for a full five minutes.'

'Stop calling him ''lover-boy'',' Angie groaned. 'His name's Lance.'

'OK. Lance what?'

'Sterling.'

'It would be. Here's the earrings.' And she held out a pair of amber and gold creations which would hang to her shoulderblades.

Angie shook her head at them. 'No, Vanessa. They're too much. I'll just wear these simple gold drops, if you don't mind.'

'I don't mind, but just remember whose earrings you were wearing when you snaffled his attention last night.'

Angie declined telling Vanessa that Lance had also thought her a tramp of the first order last night, and that maybe the saucy earrings had contributed to that first impression. 'Maybe, but that was a party. This is daytime. Oh, God, there's the doorbell.'

Vanessa swanned off towards the door while Angie fled back into the bathroom.

Her hands shook as she pinned up her hair, resulting in the haphazard style Vanessa had suggested more by accident than design. Still, she felt surprisingly satisfied with the final result. She looked classy but sexy. Cool, yet subtly sensual.

Grace Kelly, with auburn hair.

Collecting herself with several deep steadying breaths, Angie finally found the courage to leave the sanctuary of the bathroom and face her destiny.

He looked as gorgeous as Vanessa had said, his almost dazzling glamour seeming out of place in their small and cheaply furnished lounge-room. He was standing with his back to the half-open venetian blind when she entered the room, his suit jacket open, his hands slung lazily into the depths of his trouser pockets.

The slats of sunlight coming through the window glinted a line of gold on his glossy head, and picked up the silk sheen in his expensive Italian suit. His shirt was the palest blue, his tie and kerchief a bold mixture of blues and yellows and greens in a splotchy design.

The only other time Angie had seen Lance formally dressed had been at his wedding, which wasn't the same as encountering it in one's own living-room at eleven in the morning. She realised with a suddenly sinking heart that she could have bought ten of her orange linen dresses with the money it had taken to buy that suit.

Lance's wealth had never bothered her before. But then neither had she harboured this kind of hope about him before. Now she saw his multi-millionaire status as a major hurdle in their ever becoming more than just transitory lovers. Girls like Angie Brown didn't marry men like Lance Sterling. At best, they became girlfriends of a sort.

Or mistresses...

Angie realised she was standing there frowning at him, and that Lance was frowning at her frowning at him while Vanessa was frowning at them both. Carefully placing that stupid dream of hers back where it belonged, she found a plastic smile from somewhere.

'You're very punctual,' she said crisply.

'And you're very beautiful,' he returned silkily, bringing a small sigh from Vanessa's lips.

Angie glared at her, then bent to pick up her cream handbag from where it was sitting on the coffee-table. It wasn't an exact match for her cream shoes, which hadn't bothered her earlier but now did. She wished she'd gone out and bought new shoes and bag. She wished she'd bought brand new underwear. She wished her earrings were real gold and not gold-plated.

Damn it all, she almost wished she were rich!

'Shall we go?' she suggested airily.

'Nice to have met you, Vanessa,' Lance said, extending a polite hand.

Vanessa did likewise. 'And you. So where are you two off to today?' she asked before Lance could propel Angie out of the door.

Angie found herself pulling away from the possessive and highly disturbing touch on her elbow to look into those brilliant blue eyes of his. 'Yes, where are we off to today, Lance?' she echoed, amazed at how calm and casual she sounded.

Vanessa was right. She *had* developed a rather controlled façade over her years living in Sydney, and while it was a good cover for feelings best hidden she wasn't at all sure that she liked it. Where had the simpler, more honest country girl gone to? Would *she* have wanted to be rich? Would the Angie of old have felt somehow inferior because her stupid damned shoes weren't exactly the same colour as her bag?

'I thought I might take you shopping,' he said, his sensually sculptured mouth curving back into a slight smile. 'I did promise to replace your dress, remember? Then I thought we'd go somewhere for a long lunch.'

'Oh, so Angie will be back for tea, will she?' Vanessa persisted, her own smile extremely naughty. 'It's my turn to cook, you see, and I need to know if it will be for two. Or maybe three?' And she threw Lance a quizzical look.

'I wouldn't be expecting Angie home for tea,' he returned with silky smoothness, the amused gleam in his eyes showing that he knew exactly what Vanessa was up to. 'I wouldn't be expecting her till very late tonight, actually. I've also made plans for this evening. You *are* free this evening, aren't you, Angie?' he directed straight at her, cleverly bypassing Vanessa.

'Yes,' was all she could manage. Dear God, why had she agreed to Lance picking her up this early? The day stretched ahead as hour after hour of sheer torture. She wasn't even sure she would enjoy the evening, when it finally came. Maybe by then she would be too nervous.

'Excellent,' Lance pronounced. 'Goodbye, Vanessa.'

'Goodbye? That sounds like we won't be seeing each other again.' Angie flinched at the cynical implication behind Vanessa's remark.

'Does it?' Lance drawled. '*Au revoir*, then. I'm sure that won't be the case.'

'I *hope* not,' she muttered, and Angie rolled her eyes at her behind Lance's back. Vanessa responded with an immediate but patently false smile. 'Well, off you go,' she gushed. 'And don't forget what I said about drinking, Angie.'

'I won't, Vanessa,' she bit out, taking Lance's arm and practically pulling him out of the flat before that mischief-maker said another word.

Lance gave a dry chuckle once the door was shut.

'What's so funny?' Angie almost snapped.

'Your friend. Anyone would think you were Little Red Riding Hood about to venture into the woods with the big bad wolf. What on earth did you tell her about me?'

'Only the truth.'

'Your version of the truth bears little resemblance to the real truth, Angie. Not that it's your fault. Bud's been feeding you a warped view of me for years. I told him so last night. I also told him that it had to stop.'

Angie sucked in a shocked breath. 'You didn't tell him you were taking me out today, did you?'

'No, though, damn it all, I was tempted to. The only reason I didn't was because I'd promised you. Still, I knew I'd say something I'd regret if I stayed there, so I went to a motel for the night.'

Last night's visions of Lance and that blonde rolling around on a motel bed immediately flashed into her mind, and, try as she might, Angie couldn't get rid of them. *Or* the suspicion that Lance's reason for going to a motel for the night had nothing to do with a spat with Bud and everything to do with ridding himself of the frustration she herself had caused.

She continued walking down the stairs in a black silence, hating her doubts yet grabbing at them with a wild despair.

'You've gone all silent on me,' he said with a weary sigh. 'What is it, Angie? What have I done now?'

She stopped at the bottom of the stairs, gripping her handbag in tight hands as she turned to face him. 'Swear to me you didn't sleep with that blonde last night,' she cried brokenly. 'Please, Lance. Swear it!'

Angie was taken aback by the savage fury which swept into his eyes. When they heard a group of people coming down the stairs, Lance grabbed Angie's arm and bustled her outside, then over and into his car. Once he'd climbed in behind the wheel he swivelled to face her, his face full of bitter reproach.

'And if I did so swear?' he challenged. 'What would that prove? If I were the kind of person who would do that, then I would also have no compunction about lying. But if it makes you feel better, Angie, I do swear. I did not sleep with that blonde last night, or any other woman. To cover all contingencies, I also did not kiss any other woman last night,' he went on testily, 'or have sex with her, or have her go——'

'Stop!' she groaned. 'I . . . I believe you.'

'Do you, now? How nice.' Sarcasm dripped from every word and Angie cringed.

'Oh, God, Lance, I'm so sorry. Truly I am. I do believe you. I do! It's just that you're so attractive to women and I got so jealous when I saw you talking to that blonde, and... and...'

'And I'm still lumbered with my old superstud reputation,' he finished ruefully for her. 'God, but if I could only go back in time I'd go to some blasted monastery for my education rather than that uni. I have no excuses for my truly appalling behaviour during that time, except that I was a silly, spoiled young fool with more hormones than sense.

'But I *did* change in that regard, Angie. I stopped taking advantage of this empty talent I have for attracting the opposite sex. After uni I had girlfriends, not one-night stands. Helen was my only bed-partner during the year leading up to our marriage.'

'And during your marriage, Lance? Were you faithful to her?'

'I'd be lying if I said I was. But she drove me to it. She stopped sleeping with me over a year ago. I wanted her to have children, and she refused. Hell, I'd been wanting her to have children since the day we married. She compromised by saying she would have a baby after two years. Then she extended it to three. Finally, she refused altogether. I can't tell you how furious I was. She didn't trust me to use protection after that so she simply moved out of the bedroom till I supposedly came to my senses.'

'But why wasn't she on the Pill?'

Lance's laugh was cold. 'She told me it ruined her libido and made her put on weight. Like a trusting fool, I believed her. But, of course, the Pill is no protection against other hazards besides pregnancy—especially if one wants to be wildly promiscuous.'

'Helen started having affairs?'

'She'd been having them since shortly after our honeymoon. The private detective I finally hired to investigate her a couple of months ago showed me all the times and dates of her various daytime hotel assignations, dating back nearly four years. She ruthlessly but recklessly signed and paid for them all with the credit card I gave her. Sometimes, when business called me overseas, she gave the house staff time off and actually had her current lover to stay in the house with her. They made love in our marriage bed.'

Angie could only stare at Lance.

'When I showed her the report, earlier this week, she admitted she'd never loved me but thought that I would make her a very rich divorcee. At which point I left the house before I killed her. While I was gone she packed all her things and moved out.'

'Oh, my God, Lance, that's awful! And yet...almost incredible!'

'I can show you the report,' he said drily, 'if you don't believe me.'

'It's not that I don't believe you. Of course I do. I simply can't understand any woman marrying any man she doesn't love—or any woman married to you who would ever want another man.'

Now it was Lance's turn to stare, his startled eyes slowly melting as he reached over and stroked her cheek. 'You are so good for me, my darling girl. God, but if only all females were like you. If only——' He broke off to straighten, a deep frown creasing his high forehead as he appeared to drop deep into thought.

'Lance?' she asked softly at long last.

He snapped out of his reverie to smile over at her. It was the saddest smile she had ever seen Lance give anyone, and it made her heart bleed for him. People might think he had everything in life, but in fact he had nothing of real worth, if worth was measured by the values of family love and loyalty. Angie had long known that his parents had little time for him, and he didn't have any brothers or sisters. Angie suspected that his mother had stopped having children at once when she'd produced a male heir. She'd met the woman at Lance's wedding and had been struck by her cold snobbery.

Lance's wife had obviously never really loved him, either. From what Lance had said, it was likely she'd seen dollar signs from the moment she'd met the Sterling son and heir.

Angie had opened her mouth to tell him that *she* loved him, when something held her back—some last, lingering worry which whispered that to tell him of such an enduring and almost blind love would be to give him great power over her. As much as Angie did admire Lance in many ways, his moral fibre had to have been corrupted by his background, plus that ghastly marriage.

'Let's not talk about Helen any more,' she said instead. 'Let's not talk about anything serious today. Let's just have fun.'

His answering smile was much more like the Lance she remembered. His perfect teeth sparkled, his blue eyes flashed, that cheeky and charming dimple of his dimpled cheekily and with great charm.

'Best suggestion I've had all year!' he pronounced heartily.

He drove over the bridge into the city, where he turned into the driveway of the Prince Hotel—one of the new boutique establishments springing up all over Sydney. Angie only recognised the place because she'd seen a small spot about it on the television recently. Described as a classic of old-world charm and grace, it was reputed to be scandalously expensive, and patronised only by the very wealthy or the very famous. Strict privacy was what they offered, plus discretion and red carpet service.

'Er... what are we coming in here for?' Angie asked hesitantly. 'Will we be lunching here?'

'No. I'm staying here.'

'Since when?'

'Since I rang and made a booking this morning. It's supposedly within walking distance of the shops and the theatres, not to mention the quay and Darling Harbour. It should make a perfect base for our activities today.'

Activities?

Angie had heard it called a lot of things but never...'activities'. An insane little giggle threatened to burst from her lips but she smothered it just in time and gave Lance what she hoped was a perfectly unreadable look. She must have succeeded for he frowned at her, the kind of frown a man gave a woman when he didn't know what was going on in her mind but would dearly have loved to.

'I thought you said you wanted to have fun,' he muttered. 'If that's the case, do you think you might try smiling at me?'

She did, and when he smiled back a warm wave of love rushed through her.

'That's better,' he said in a satisfied tone. 'Come on. Let's get out and go inside. The valet wants to park the car.'

Angie was all eyes as she climbed out, standing there gazing all around her while Lance instructed the pompously uniformed porter about his bag then gave the equally pompously uniformed valet his car keys. 'Have you stayed here before?' she whispered as Lance took her arm and guided her through the heavy glass doors.

'No. Never. And why are you whispering?'

'This is a whispering sort of place,' she said, still in hushed tones, at the same time glancing all around her with wide-eyed fascination at the rich wood-panelled walls, the plush red-carpeted floor, the deep leather chairs and the many bronze statues—all of old-fashioned-looking ladies in various stages of undress. Angie found the décor a little much, and while she could imagine a lot of men liking it, she didn't think it reflected Lance's taste. 'Er...why did you choose it?'

'Because it was the only hotel in Sydney where the honeymoon suite wasn't booked out for tonight.'

Angie ground to a halt, her stomach fluttering. 'The...the honeymoon suite?' She stared up at Lance, searching his face for an explanation.

'That's right,' he said, his voice as softly caressing as his eyes. 'I decided our first night together required something really special—something reflective of how I think about you and what you mean to me.'

A great lump filled her throat. Tears threatened, but she valiantly battled them away. 'That...that's very sweet of you, Lance.'

His low laugh had a drily cynical note to it. 'It's not sweet at all, Angie. I haven't been brought up to be sweet. I'm selfish and arrogant, and at times utterly ruthless. I'm pulling out all the stops to make sure you never forget tonight. Or me. If you thought I'd spoilt you for other men before then, believe me, by tomorrow morning you're going to be well and truly spoilt for other men for the rest of your life! Now, sit down over in that armchair,' he ordered, smiling an utterly ruthless but devastatingly attractive smile. 'I'm going over to check in. Then I'm taking you shopping!'

CHAPTER NINE

'YES, we'll take that one too,' Lance said from where he was sitting in a comfy winged chair, supervising Angie's try-ons and sipping the cup of coffee the staff had brought him. They were in a very exclusive fashion boutique in the Centrepoint Building where, naturally, Lance had been given first class treatment from the moment he walked in with Angie in tow. He was that kind of man.

Angie frowned, knowing that the gold brocade suit she was wearing cost a small fortune—much more than the black velvet dinner dress he'd just given the nod to. Angie had not minded the velvet number, as Lance *had* ruined her green silk dress last night and it wasn't too expensive. When he'd suggested she try on the brocade outfit, which had been highlighted in the display in the window, she had done so, thinking he was giving her an alternative choice to the velvet.

In truth, she *did* prefer it. The sleek straight skirt and hour-glass-style jacket suited her longish body to perfection, and the lowish V-neckline between the satin-edged lapels showed off her nice bust to advantage. Angie had fallen in love with it, till she glanced at the price tag in the changing-room.

Still frowning, she walked over to Lance and bent down to whisper in his ear. 'Lance . . . this suit is very, very expensive. I couldn't possibly let you buy it for me.'

He replaced the coffee-cup in the saucer with a small sigh. 'Yes, you can,' he told her firmly, though in a discreetly low voice. 'You can do anything you want, Angie; *have* anything you want. You're with me today as my woman, and I am a very rich man. Indulge me, my darling. Let me pamper you and spoil you. It will give me great pleasure to dress you—almost as much as it will give me to undress you this evening.' This last remark was made with a not so discreet glance at the shadowed valley between her breasts.

Angie blushed fiercely as her head jerked up and their eyes met. 'You...you shouldn't say things like that,' she said, shaken by his calling her his darling, and very shaken by the images his other words had catapulted into her mind. A wicked heat started firing her blood and flushing her skin. Desire quickly became a throbbing pulse in her veins.

His smile was vaguely triumphant. 'Perhaps not,' he drawled. 'But I simply couldn't resist. I've never been with a female before who would react as you just did. It's enchanting. But then you *are* enchanting, sweet Angie. In every way...'

'I...I asked you not to call me that,' she said, trying to sound stern, but failing miserably.

'But why, when it suits you?'

He smiled, and she couldn't help it. She smiled back. 'You're a wicked man, Lance Sterling.'

'Well, you can't have everything, darling. Rich and good just don't go together.'

A fact which she'd already realised. Angie wondered if he was paving the way to turning her into his mistress. Perhaps he was already corrupting her, getting her used to things she could never afford but which he could continue to give to her provided she continued to give him what she would give him tonight.

'I'm not going to become your mistress, Lance,' she said, hoping that saying the words out loud would prevent the reality happening.

He seemed taken aback. 'Is that what you think this is?' And he waved down her expensively clad body with his free hand.

'Would I be wrong?' she challenged.

'You would,' he said sharply, but did not elaborate.

Angie's surprise quickly turned to bewilderment. 'Then, what is it?'

'It's fun, Angie.' He smiled an engaging though enigmatic smile. 'What you said you wanted today.'

'Fun,' she repeated blankly, till the penny suddenly dropped. Yes, of course! How silly of her! Nothing so serious and semi-permanent as making her his mistress.

Tonight, for all Lance's softly seductive words, was really just a one-night stand, dressed up to look like something else. His arrogant claim that he would spoil her for any other man was just that. An arrogant claim. It contained no promise of tomorrows. It contained nothing but the promise of a night she would never forget.

But oh, dear heaven, how she was looking forward to that night. Even now, as she gazed down at the handsome man draped elegantly over the chair before her, she wanted to beg him to stop this fiasco, to take her back to that honeymoon suite immediately. She did not want to waste another moment of her short time with him being dressed up like some Barbie doll, or eating a stupid lunch she had no stomach for.

'What if I told you I'm not finding this much fun?' she choked out. 'What if I told you that I'd much rather we... That I'd prefer to... That I want you to...to...' Her voice trailed away as she simply could not confess the desire now running rampant through her. But she must have still conveyed the shameful truth to him by her flushed cheeks and glittering eyes, by the way her lips stayed softly apart to allow the shallow panting caused by her rapidly beating heart to escape.

He stared up at her over the rim of the cup, holding her captive with his eyes and thrilling her with the sudden passion which blazed away in their brilliant blue depths. It was as though her bumbling confession had stripped away the cavalier façade he'd been wearing all day, and suddenly she saw what making love to her meant to him. She was both incredibly moved and incredibly turned on.

'Lance,' she breathed shakily, everything around him going out of focus, as it had the previous evening.

'Yes,' he rasped back. 'I know.' The cup clattered back into the saucer once more, and he seemed to have to drag his eyes away from her before rising slowly to his feet. 'The lady will take the outfit she has on,' he told the hovering saleslady in a brusquely commanding voice. 'She won't be changing back into her other clothes. Wrap her orange dress up with the black one. Here's my credit card.'

When he turned back to Angie she was actually trembling. A mixture of nerves and excitement had taken hold of her, making her feel sick with anticipation of what was to come. There was something incredibly thrilling about the unknown. Yet also something incredibly frightening.

When she flashed Lance a torn look, he took her arm within a steadying grip and steered her over to the sales desk. Five minutes later he was bundling her into a taxi for the short ride back to his hotel.

He seemed to know not to speak to her during this brief journey, or in the hotel lobby, or even on the lift ride which carried them up to the honeymoon suite. Angie was grateful for his silence, aware that she was incapable of making sensible conversation at that moment.

The lift doors opened, and before she knew it she was standing at a heavy wooden door while Lance inserted the key into its brass lock. For the first time her mind turned to what the honeymoon suite might look like. She wasn't sure what to expect after the décor downstairs, but it wasn't what met her eyes when Lance pushed open the door and ushered her inside.

Everything was white or cream or gold. White walls and furniture, cream carpet and curtains, gold lamps and cushions. There was quite a bit of glass too. All the table-tops were glass. One whole wall was glass, with a splendid view of the harbour bridge and surrounds. A huge crystal and gold chandelier hung from the ornately plastered and very high ceiling.

'Oh!' she gasped on entering, all carnal desire momentarily pushed to one side. 'What a lovely room!'

It was more than just a lovely room. It was a honeymoon suite to exceed all honeymoon suites. Gracious. Spacious. And touchingly romantic. Angie moved in somewhat of a daze through the large sitting-area into the dream of a bedroom. She stared at the huge white four-poster bed, with its flouncy lace valance, the pearly satin quilted spread and the multitude of small lacy cushions propped up against the four satin-covered pillows. Truly a bed fit for a bride on her wedding-night.

'You like it?' Lance said softly, coming up from behind her and curving his hands over her shoulders.

'It . . . it's exquisite,' she managed to get out in a strangled tone. Oh, God, she wasn't ready for this. She'd thought she was but she wasn't. She was petrified. Almost literally! She felt like a frozen piece of wood. Or a statue.

'Try to relax,' Lance suggested softly, and bent to kiss her on the neck.

Angie stiffened even further. 'I . . . I need to use the bathroom.'

Lance's lips left her constricted throat and she practically fled into the bathroom, shutting the door behind her.

For a long moment she leant against the door, her eyes shut, her heart thudding. When at last she opened her eyes it was to take in the largest bathroom Angie had ever seen. And the most opulent. Great expanses of creamy gold-veined marble, with three vanity bowls, an enormous shower, a sunken spa bath, plus a matching toilet and bidet.

She shook her head at the gold taps which were in the shape of cupids, the water being shot out of their arrows. She was also stunned by all the other provisions. Every conceivable complimentary item was supplied, from 'his and her' hairdryers, to toiletries, toothbrushes and tissues. A telephone hung on the wall next to the toilet. The towels and robes were plush and white, small satin cupids embroidered on various corners and pockets.

This was not a honeymoon suite for any old Darby and Joan from Woop-Woop, Angie conceded. This was a honeymoon suite for a multimillionaire. One night here would cost a mint.

A new burst of nerves really did necessitate a brief using of the toilet and bidet, after which Angie got a grip on herself and returned to the living-area. There, she was amazed to find Lance in the process of filling two crystal flutes from a bottle of champagne. An elaborate silver ice-bucket was resting on a side-table, along with a huge platter of assorted fruits, cheeses and crackers. None of these things had been there, Angie was fairly certain, when they'd come in.

Or had she just not seen them? Had she been so full of blind passion when she'd first walked in that she'd been oblivious to such minor details? It was possible. She'd been ready for anything back then. Now, the time delay, plus a resurgence of nerves, was dampening her desires, making her worry that she might make a fool of herself.

Lance had had so many beautiful women—all undoubtedly more experienced than herself. His wife had been absolutely gorgeous—a young Elizabeth Taylor, with black hair, creamy skin and wide violet eyes. Helen's ultimately proving to be a slut did not lessen the fact that she must have known everything there was to know about pleasing a man in the bedroom. Lance would not have married her if he hadn't been very satisfied in that regard.

'All this came while you were in the bathroom,' he said, looking up and holding one of the flutes out to her. 'Compliments of the hotel.'

'Oh.' Angie was relieved that she hadn't been so besotted that she'd failed to see something so obvious. She also remembered what Vanessa had said about having a couple of drinks to relax before the big event, and came forward to take the proffered glass.

Lance smiled as he clinked her glass with his. 'To my beautiful bride,' he toasted, and everything inside her contracted anew, her own glass freezing in mid-air.

'Don't,' she whispered, her eyes dropping away to the floor lest he see the sudden tears pricking behind the lids.

'Don't, what?' he asked, a dark puzzlement in his voice.

'Don't make fun of me...of this...'

He swore, and her blurred gaze flew up to meet his stormy one. But once he'd witnessed her very real distress, he groaned. 'You think I would do that? There is no fun in this moment, Angie, only a very deep regret that I have waited this long. I should have done this years ago,' he murmured, curling his free hand round her neck and gently caressing it. His eyes moved from hers to her trembling mouth, then back down to where her breasts were rising and falling in a raggedly syncopated rhythm.

'God, but you *are* incredibly beautiful,' he said thickly, putting his own glass down and taking hers from her oddly frozen fingers. Odd, because the rest of her was quivering madly. 'I don't deserve you,' he said. 'But that's irrelevant at this vital stage. I must drink of this cup...' And he took a sip of the champagne. 'And so must you...'

He held the glass to her lips till they parted, then tipped a little of the champagne inside, watching her through narrowed eyes as she swallowed, then as her tongue darted forward to lick up an escaping droplet.

'More,' he commanded huskily, and pressed the glass back to her lips, his hands shaking slightly. The crystal rim tinkled against her teeth, and her hands fluttered up to enclose his, both of them trembling as she helped him to tip more of the sparkling liquid into her mouth.

Angie had never experienced anything as blisteringly sensual as the feel of the champagne filling her mouth and throat, before she was forced to gulp it down. After the first swallow Lance filled her mouth anew, the action repeated till not one but both glasses were empty and Angie's senses were spinning. The champagne had hit her empty stomach with a quite savage force, fizzing into her bloodstream with incredible speed. She began to tingle all over, swaying on her high heels. Lance put the second glass back down, then scooped her up into his arms.

'My hero,' she said, then shuddered with a type of surrender.

He didn't say a word, simply carried her into the bedroom and laid her down on the snow-white quilt. She closed her eyes when he sat beside her on the bed and started undressing her. Her head—and the room—had begun to spin slightly. Not that she felt sick at all. She felt glorious, and very, very accommodating.

When he told her to sit up, she sat up. When he told her to lift her bottom, she lifted her bottom. When he told her to lie back down, she lay back down.

It was only when she was down to her strapless
bra and panties, and he appeared to have abandoned her, that her eyes flew open. But it seemed
he'd only stopped to begin taking off his own
clothes. His jacket and tie had been already dis-
carded; his shirt was hanging open to the waist.

Their eyes locked—Angie's blinking, his guarded.
'You feeling OK?' he asked.

'I'm not sure,' she admitted, aware the room was
not entirely steady.

'You'll be fine in a minute or two. You drank
that champagne too quickly.'

'You made me,' she accused.

'Yeah, right, Angie. Just as I made you come
here.' He smiled a wry smile, then stripped off the
shirt, giving her an unimpeded view of the same
beautiful bare chest which had fascinated her all
those years ago.

Her mouth went dry as she contemplated its glorious contours, from the width of his shoulders to
his well-defined chest muscles and the washboard
flatness of his stomach. The thought that shortly
she would be able to run her hands at will over his
body sent little tremors running through her. Her
nipples peaked hard inside her bra, poking at the
cream satin which confined them.

Lance's gaze zeroed in on them as though they
had red lights built in. Seemingly entranced, he sat
down next to her, his right hand reaching out to
take possession of the closest peak between his
thumb and forefinger. Angie's eyes widened as he
rolled the nipple left and right. Such an action might

have been painful if she'd been naked, but the nipple's satin covering softened the feeling to an exquisitely sharp sensation. When he squeezed gently, Angie betrayed her pleasure with a deeply sensual moan.

His right hand moved over to her other breast while his left took over with the already sensitised peak, and Angie sucked in a strangled breath at the doubled delight. When he slipped his thumbs under the bra to rub across her naked nipples her back arched away from the bed, her lips gasping apart.

He bent to cover those lips with his, sending his tongue between them, stunning her with his wildly urgent thrusting. Till then, he'd seemed so controlled, but now, suddenly, his own desire was off the leash.

Angie's body leapt with an answering savagery of her own. Her hands reached up to clasp tightly around his neck, keeping his lips hard upon hers, keeping that devouring tongue deep within her mouth. She thrilled to his moan of raw response, to the way he roughly rid her of her bra while he kissed her, his hands wonderfully brutal on her bare breasts. She didn't want him to be gentle with her. She wanted him wild!

When he finally tore his gasping mouth from hers, she groaned her disappointment. But she wasn't disappointed for long. His lips swept down her throat to her aching breasts, where he punished the already aching tips with broad sweeps of his tongue, giving each nipple a brief but barbaric

suckling before abandoning them to move further
down her body.

His mouth traced a feverish though tantalising
path as he peeled her panties down her legs, kissing
and licking her skin as he went but deliberately
avoiding that molten area between her thighs.

But, despite his teasing, Angie knew what was
coming, memories of the night before in the car
making her stomach tighten in anticipation, a fierce
heat racing through her veins as she recalled how
it had felt when his mouth had made love to her
down there. She would never forget the delicious
screaming of each nerve-ending as he'd sucked on
her most sensitive spot. She wanted to experience
that screaming again. She longed for the wildly tormenting tension, the electrifyingly sharp sensations, the utterly addictive torture.

Tossing her panties aside at long last, he began
working his way back up her legs, but this time
with his hands only. To begin with, Angie felt
slightly disappointed—she wanted his mouth—but
by the time he reached the soft flesh of her inner
thighs her heart was beating like a threshing ma-
chine. With a merciless and devastating expertise,
he explored the moist valley between her thighs,
teasing and tormenting her till her legs fell wider
and wider apart, wanting more...asking for
more...aching for more. Her eyes grew heavy with
desire, the lids fluttering half closed on a low moan.

When his touch finally probed at her virgin en-
trance, her buttocks instinctively clenched tightly
together. They lifted slightly from the bed, pressing

herself with wanton abandon against his fingertips, inviting a deeper penetration. He obliged and she accepted him avidly, without hesitation, without discomfort.

Where she'd resisted last night, clamping her muscles in rejection, now she flowered open, wallowing in the less painful and much less threatening penetration. In fact, she could not get enough. When his mouth unexpectedly joined in, his tongue homing in on the swollen apex of her desire, everything quickly spiralled out of control and over the edge. Spasm after spasm racked her body, making her cry out, making her head thrash from side to side on the pillow.

It was the most intense, most incredible experience she had ever lived through, but it was over much too quickly. Her eyes flew open on a groan of dismay when his mouth and hands immediately abandoned her, leaving her lying there, awash with a mixture of ambivalent feelings. As much as her orgasm had been glorious, it was not really what she'd wanted. She'd wanted him joined to her, deep inside her, climaxing with her.

When Lance went to stand up, she sat bolt-upright and clutched at his arm, the desire to be as one with him still incredibly strong. There was an emptiness within her body and her soul that only he could fill.

'Don't leave me,' she cried.

He returned to kiss her trembling mouth and laid her back against the pillows. 'My sweet Angie,' he murmured. 'I'm not leaving you. I'm just going to undress.'

'Oh . . . oh, all right, then. But don't be long.'

'I'm not going anywhere. While you're waiting,' he added, smiling wryly, 'select one of these!' And he drew several small foil packets from his trouser pocket and dropped them nonchalantly on to her naked stomach. 'I couldn't make up my mind which kind might take your fancy so I brought one of each.'

His naturalness totally defused any embarrassment in Angie. She picked up each one in turn, the last one making her eyes snap up to his. '*Passion-fruit* flavoured?'

He grinned wickedly while he unzipped his trousers. 'It seemed an appropriate flavour. Besides, I seem to recall you were very partial to passion-fruit.'

Now Angie *did* colour with embarrassment. And perhaps something else. She knew she wouldn't need any incentive to do whatever would please him. She couldn't wait to explore his body as he'd explored hers, to kiss and possess every inch of him, to make him shudder with desire for her.

At last he was naked, and he was as magnificent as she'd known he would be, and wonderfully uninhibited about being nude before her, despite his intense arousal. He returned to sit beside her, dispensing with all the condoms but one, then doing what he had to do with a stunningly swift expertise which left Angie floundering. Before she could feel any real dismay, however, he bent to kiss her mouth

again, caressing her body at the same time till she
was trembling with desire for him.

'Now, close your eyes, my darling,' he whispered
into her softened lips. 'Lie back and think of
nothing but you and me, together in each other's
arms, loving each other. We've both waited for this
for a long time, and you deserve the very best...'

His words had the most powerful effect on her.
Her love for him rose to fill her heart to overflowing. She reached for him, pulling him down,
on to and into her body. Her cry was a cry of pure
joy, despite the flash of pain. When he hesitated,
she clung to him, pulling him deeper and deeper,
till they indeed were one.

For a long moment they stayed that way, their
mouths searching for each other to complete their
union, their hearts beating to the same beat. He
speared her fingers with his and lifted her hands
high above her, stretching their upper bodies full-
length till he covered every inch of her chest and
arms with his. Again, he stayed that way for several
moments, and she gloried in his weight upon her,
a feeling of warm surrender washing through her.

When he began to move within her, her legs lifted
automatically, to wrap high around him so that he
might sink even more deeply into her, and quite
instinctively she began to move with him. Their
rhythm became a drum-beat, first in her head, then
all through her body. *She* became the drum,
stretched   tighter   and   tighter,   and   Lance
the drummer.

Soon the beat grew louder and faster. Angie became hotter and hotter, beads of perspiration breaking out all over her body. She feared everything inside her might burst if Lance didn't slow down, or stop. Then something did explode, deep within her, and suddenly everything was very, very right.

She cried out, and clung to him all the harder as spasms of the most exquisite delight racked her insides. They went on and on, squeezing and releasing Lance, till he too cried out. Angie felt the great shudders of his climax, and tears sprang to her eyes. Perhaps they were tears of release and relief, but she liked to think that they were tears of love. For she did so love this man who had just made the most beautiful love to her. Loved him so much that to contemplate life without him was unendurable.

Now the tears flowed fresh, and Lance was kissing them from her face, cradling her to him and stroking her back.

'Don't cry, my darling,' he told her. 'You were wonderful. You *are* wonderful. God, I wish I didn't have to go back to Melbourne tomorrow. I wish I could stay here and make love to you forever.'

CHAPTER TEN

ANGIE froze momentarily in his arms before sighing her resignation to his words. Lance's voicing the transitory nature of their affair should not have shocked or distressed her, since she'd known the reality all along. But it *was* hard to reconcile reality with what they had just shared. To Angie it had been an out-of-this-world experience—so damned wonderful, in fact, that she'd begun to harbour stupid hopes again, romantic fool that she was!

She sighed again, and Lance's head lifted.

'Are they sighs of satisfaction, exhaustion, or something else?' he asked.

She smiled softly and reached up to comb his hair back from his forehead with her fingers. 'What do you think?' she said.

'I don't know,' came his pensive answer. 'That's why I'm asking.'

Angie felt slightly flustered by the question, a nervous laugh escaping from her lips. She foresaw their having an argument if she started telling him how much she loved him, and how much she wanted to be a part of his life on an ongoing basis. If all she was ever going to have with Lance was the rest of today and tonight, she wasn't about to do or say anything to spoil their short time together.

'All three, I guess,' she said. 'I'm very satisfied, very exhausted, but also very disappointed.' This last bit she delivered with a softly seductive pout.

It threw him. 'Disappointed?'

'Yes. I'd like you to be able to stay and make love to me forever too. But if you have to go back to Melbourne tomorrow then that's that. We still have the rest of today and tonight, don't we? Gosh, Lance, I wouldn't have left it this long if I'd known sex was so fantastic. Though perhaps it's the man I'm with who's fantastic. You're an incredible lover—do you know that?'

He was frowning down at her and she wondered what she'd said that was wrong. He muttered something under his breath, then abruptly withdrew, making her gasp. Desolation swept in at the empty feeling he left behind, not just in her body but in her soul. Her heart sank ever further when he rolled from her, stood up, then strode off into the bathroom.

Clearly she'd said something to offend him. But what?

The blackest depression descended while she listened to the bathroom sounds—the flushing of the toilet, then the turning on of taps. But when the taps remained on, she began to frown. When Lance wrenched the door open, standing there naked and glowering, she sat up. 'What is it?' she said. 'What have I done? Why are you mad at me?'

'Well you might ask,' he growled, and stalked over to haul her unceremoniously up and over his shoulder like a sack of potatoes. 'We're going to have a spa bath together, Angie Brown. And while we're in there, we're going to talk.'

'Talk?' she squeaked, all the breath having been knocked out of her body.

'Yeah, *talk*, lover,' he snarled as he carried her into the bathroom, both his arms clamped firmly around her thighs and buttocks. 'What did you think? That you'd add an underwater screw to your tally of new experiences for today? Perhaps you'd like me to screw you in the shower as well, or on the floor, or up against the vanity? Mirrors can add a real dimension to sex, you know. Oh, yes, I forgot... We still have the passion-fruit-flavoured experience to go as well. Hell, I'm really looking forward to that one. Make it good and I'll dash out for some strawberry as well!'

'Why, you... you...' She began to pummel his bare buttocks with balled fists. 'I'll have you know that——'

She broke off with a squeal when he dragged her off him and dumped her into the hot frothing bath, bubbles and water splashing up the walls and on to the floor.

'You'll have me know what?' he ground out, plonking himself down in the furthest corner of the bath away from her and crossing his arms.

Angie glared at him over the expanse between them. 'You're a damned hypocrite, Lance Sterling,' she stated, lifting her chin in cool outrage. 'It's all right for you to have sown your wild oats but I'm not even allowed one night's wild oats without your looking down your nose at me.'

'That's right. Because you're *not* me. You're my sweet Angie, and I want you to stay that way.'

'Oh, piffle!'

'*Piffle*?' he bellowed.

'Yes, *piffle*!' she repeated, just as loudly, folding her arms as well and curling her top lip at him. 'I've never heard such a load of rubbish in my whole life! You were all for bringing me here and deflowering me, Lance, and now, suddenly, just because I really liked it and want a whole lot more, you've gone all prim and proper. What is it? Conscience getting the better of you all of a sudden? Or are you just sorry that you have to go back to Melbourne and some other man might get the benefit of your splendid initiation?'

'You're not to sleep with any other man,' he growled. '*Ever*!'

'Really? And how do you aim to stop me?'

'By making you my wife!'

Angie was staggered, as much by Lance's unexpected announcement as by her immediate and furious rejection of the idea. 'And what makes you imagine that I'd even *consider* marrying you?'

'Because you love me!' he said, blue eyes blazing.

No mention of his loving her, she noted bitterly.

That's because he doesn't, that dark voice in her head whispered. His offer of marriage is just a means to an end. You in his bed. Exclusively.

Her laugh carried disbelief at his presumptuous arrogance. 'You have to be joking. As I said last night, Lance, how could I possibly love a man I

don't even know? I had a crush on you once, and
there's still a chemistry between us. But that's not
love.'

'Who says it isn't?'

'Well, even if it *is* a form of love—and I question
that—it's not the kind which lasts. It's certainly not
the kind that makes a good foundation for
marriage.'

'Is that your final answer?'

Was it? Panic raced in as the reality of what she
was doing hit her. The man she loved had asked
her to marry him and she'd just turned him down.
Her indecision turned to anguish. How *could* she
blindly commit her life to Lance when what she'd
said was true? She didn't know him. Not as yet,
anyway.

Gathering all her common sense and courage, she
ground out, 'For now, it is.'

'And in the future?'

She swallowed convulsively. 'That's up to you,
Lance. You might try working on winning my love
and letting me get to know you better. I'm sure
what I feel for you could easily turn to true love,
given the chance.'

'I see,' he said thoughtfully.

'Do *you* love *me*?' she asked, and held
her breath.

Their eyes clashed and his face hardened. 'I'm
not in the habit of telling women I love them after
they've just rejected me.'

'But I haven't rejected you. I've told you to work at winning me, if you really want me. The trouble with you, Lance, is that you've had everything given to you on a silver platter. You must learn that some things don't come easily.'

'You were pretty easy today,' he snapped.

'And so were you,' she countered.

They glared at each other and slowly, very slowly, Lance's mouth curved back into a smile. 'You're turned into a tough little cookie, haven't you?'

'No, Lance, I've just grown up.'

'And very nicely too,' he said, his eyes dropping to her breasts, which weren't totally covered by the bubbles. Angie was irritated to feel her nipples respond. She gulped when Lance closed the distance between them, stiffening when he curled a soapy hand around her neck and started drawing her mouth towards his.

'What...what do you think you're doing?' she said, despising her voice for shaking on her.

'Exactly what you told me to do. I'm setting about winning you.'

'And you think this is the way?'

'Hell, Angie, a man has to use whatever limited talents he's got in a situation like this. You yourself said I was an incredible lover. I guess I have to believe you, because my Angie wouldn't lie. She's as honest as the day is long...'

The fingers caressing her throat gradually exerted enough pressure to close the small distance between their mouths. It was a lightly teasing, impossibly tantalising kiss, an annoyingly effective kiss. Angie yanked her head back and he chuckled ruefully. 'Hopefully, this day will prove to be *very* long, because I can see I've still got a lot of winning to do...'

Angie lay in bed on her side, watching Lance's chest rise and fall in the steady rhythm of sleep. Her own chest rose, then fell in a weary sigh. The light trickling through the curtained window showed that dawn wasn't very far away.

'Well, Lance,' she murmured to his unconscious form. 'You've won. I know now I can't risk letting you go back to Melbourne today without me, can't risk your never asking me to marry you a second time, can't risk that I might never lie like this with you again...'

She sighed another soul-shattering sigh and rolled on to her back, fearful of her future if she married this man. Would he be faithful to her? Would he make a good father? Would he share his life with her in every way, like her father did with her mother?

For that was what she wanted. Not an empty high society marriage, where the wife was little better than a social hostess. She also wanted her children always with her, not sent off to some toffee-nosed boarding-school. She definitely wanted her husband to come home every night, not to be jetting off all the time on so-called overseas business trips.

Angie accepted unhappily that she might never have all that if she became Mrs Lance Sterling. The kind of marriage he would offer her would probably prove to be hell. But not to become Lance's wife would be condemning herself to an even worse hell.

She closed her eyes and contemplated that alternative fate. Never to feel his arms around her again, or his lips on hers, or his body blended with hers. Never to hear the wonderfully seductive words he'd whispered to her over and over.

'You're so beautiful...I adore you...I've always wanted you...I'll always want you...I'm crazy about you...'

Lance had undoubtedly pulled out all the stops each time they'd made love during the long day and the long, long night. He'd spent limitless time on foreplay, always making sure that she was so aroused by the time they moved on that she would agree to whatever demands he'd made of her, and whatever position he'd suggested. When his supply of protection had been exhausted he hadn't stopped making love to her, he'd simply stopped seeking satisfaction for himself. He had seemed to gain as much pleasure from seeing her climax as from having one himself, although, in hindsight, Angie doubted that was so. It had simply been his way of corrupting her further to his will. Of totally seducing, then winning her.

And how well he'd succeeded, she conceded with bittersweet realisation. She'd told him proudly that some things would not come easily. What a laugh that was! She obviously hadn't anticipated her own sexual weaknesses.

The sound of the telephone ringing beside the bed startled her. Who could it be? The only person who knew she was here was Vanessa, Angie having called her flatmate the previous evening to tell her where she was and that she wouldn't be home that night. Vanessa hadn't sounded at all surprised, though Angie had been relieved that Vanessa was on her way out on a date and didn't have time for more questions.

'Answer it,' Lance mumbled beside her. 'Maybe the hotel's on fire.'

Angie reached for the receiver. 'Yes?' she said, a frown on her face and in her voice.

'That you, Angie?'

Bud! Oh, God, it was Bud! Angie clamped her hand on the phone and groaned.

'Who is it?' Lance immediately demanded, propping himself up on one elbow.

'Bud,' was all she could manage.

Lance's swear-word told it all.

Angie gulped and lifted her hand. 'Yes, it's me,' she said simply.

'Gees, Angie, I couldn't believe it when Vanessa told me where you were and with whom. I can't tell you how disappointed I am in you, and how disgusted I am with Lance.'

Angie's mind began racing. Vanessa would never have told Bud where she was and with whom unless there was a real emergency. Certainly not at this hour of the morning. She would have made up some excuse for her friend. 'Never mind the lecture, Bud,' Angie said impatiently. 'What's happened? What's wrong?'

'Mum's had a heart attack,' he said bluntly.

Everything inside of Angie seized up with shock. Her mother had had a heart attack? But she was only forty-eight years old. It didn't seem possible.

A sick pounding began in her temples, and her heart.

'She... she's not dead, is she? God, Bud, don't tell me she's dead,' she cried.

'No. She's not dead. But she's in hospital. Dad says it's still touch and go.'

Angie broke down in a flood of tears, Lance taking the receiver out of her suddenly shaking hands.

'This is Lance, Bud,' she heard him say. 'Angie's too upset to talk. What's all this about?'

Angie still could not believe it. Her mother... maybe dying. What would she do if she died? What would Bud do? And Dad? Dear God, Dad wouldn't be able to cope. Not at this stage. It was too soon. A hundred years too soon!

'For pity's sake grow up, Bud, and get your priorities right,' Lance suddenly snapped. 'What in hell does it matter if Angie and I spent the night together when your mother might be dying? Now, get your butt into your car and start driving up there. And don't damned well speed! It won't do your dad any good if you wrap your stupid bloody neck around a tree.'

Angie blinked at the forceful tone in Lance's voice. She was surprised, and impressed, despite everything. He was normally so easygoing and laid back in his dealings with Bud. Crises sometimes brought out the best or the worst in people. It was clearly bringing out the best in Lance.

'No, don't waste time coming in here to pick Angie up,' he resumed, in that same masterful tone. 'I'll drive her up there myself. And you'll keep your mouth shut about Angie and me if you know what's good for you. If you say one derogatory word about us to your parents, I'll skin you alive. You've pushed our friendship as far as I can take it this weekend, Bud, and I won't take any more!'

He reached over Angie and slammed the receiver down, his tough expression melting at the sight of her tear-stained face. 'My poor darling,' he crooned, taking her in his arms and rocking her gently back and forth. 'I know what your mother means to you...to all of you. She's a grand woman.'

Angie was touched by his sympathy, and had to battle not to break into further sobs. Eventually, and reluctantly, she extricated herself from the comfort of his embrace.

'You...you'll really drive me all the way up there, Lance?' she asked. 'Don't you have to go back to Melbourne today?'

'I should, but I'm not going to. How could I possibly leave you at a time like this? You need me, Angie.'

Her eyes filled again. 'Yes . . . yes, I do. Lance, I——'

'No,' he cut in abruptly. 'Don't say any more. This isn't the right time. You're all emotional at the moment, and what you feel might not be real. Now, pop up and have a shower, love, and I'll order us some breakfast. I dare say you'll want to drop in at your flat on the way through to pick up some clothes, so shake a leg. Time might be of the essence.'

Lance's last remark sent Angie's mind flying back to her mother, lying ill and possibly dying in hospital. The thought that she might never see her mother alive again sent her hurrying out of bed and into the bathroom.

Less than an hour later, she was letting herself into her flat. As she walked into the living room the clock on the wall said twenty-five past six.

'Is that you, Angie?' Vanessa called from the bedroom.

'Yes. It's only me.'

Vanessa appeared, bleary-eyed and nightie-clad. 'I...I hope you're not mad at me,' she said worriedly. 'I wasn't going to tell that pompous brother of yours where you were, but when he told me about your mother I just had to.'

'Of course you did.'

'Where's Lance?'

'He's waiting for me in the car. He's going to drive me up home.'

'I suppose this isn't the right time to ask you how it went with you two?'

'No,' Angie returned stiffly. 'It isn't.'

Vanessa nodded. 'Is there anything I can get you? A cup of coffee or anything?'

'No, nothing.'

'I hope your mum pulls through,' she said, hovering while Angie stripped off and pulled on some white shorts and a black and white striped top.

'I hope so too,' she said, slipping her feet into a pair of black sandals.

'She always sounds so nice on the phone.'

'She is.'

'My mum's a right bitch, and I still love her.'

Angie's chin started to wobble.

Vanessa came forward and put her arms around her. 'It's all right, sweetheart. Cry. You don't have to be brave around me.'

Angie cried.

Ten minutes later, she was back in Lance's car and they were speeding north.

CHAPTER ELEVEN

'WHAT exactly do you do, Lance?'

His blue eyes whipped round at her question. They'd been travelling in virtual silence for nearly an hour, the only sound in the car some faint music from the radio.

'You don't have to talk for the sake of talking,' he said, returning his eyes to the road ahead.

'I realise that. I want to know. Bud told me once you worked in the export division of Sterling Industries. But what exactly does that entail?'

He slid her a sharp glance. 'Then you don't know?'

'Know what?'

'I moved on from that position twelve months ago. I now run Sterling Industries. I'm the managing director.'

Angie blinked her astonishment. 'No. I didn't know. I...I naturally thought your father occupied that position.'

'He did. Theoretically. Unfortunately, he hadn't been a hands-on CEO for many years, and Sterling Industries was beginning to suffer. His choosing to live in Sydney wasn't conducive to good management, considering all the companies' head offices are in Melbourne. But that was my mother's doing. She refused to live in Melbourne, and what she wanted, she got. By the time I took over, Dad's neglect plus the recent recession had put some areas of the business into deep trouble. I've been lucky enough to turn things around and we're now in a position to take advantage of the growing economy.'

Angie was both surprised and impressed. 'So how did you come to take over, Lance? Did you talk your dad into taking early retirement?'

'No. He died.'

Angie sucked in a shocked breath.

'It was in all the papers,' he added. 'The business section, that is.'

'I don't read the business section very often,' she murmured.

'I had no idea you didn't know. Bud knew, because he rang me at the time. I presumed he must have told you.'

'No. He didn't. He never mentioned it. Oh, God, I... I'm so sorry, Lance. You must have thought me very rude for not contacting you, or sending a card or something. How did your dad die? Had he been ill?' She recalled a tall, handsome man at Lance's wedding who'd not looked a day over fifty, although he had probably been older.

'Yes. Very ill. He had cancer of the pancreas and liver. There was nothing the doctors could do. He died less than three months after the original diagnosis.'

'How awful for you all. Your poor mother must have been devastated.'

'Oh, absolutely,' came his caustic reply. 'So devastated that she had to take herself off around the world to recover—her trip starting the day after the funeral. Last month she became Mrs Jonathon Winthrop the third. Fortunately, for me, Mr Winthrop lives in Texas, and can't travel due to some rare blood disease he has. I would say the next time I see my darling mama will be at my new step-papa's funeral. Though maybe not,' he added with savage sarcasm. 'If I'm a minute or two late I'll probably miss her. She'll have moved on by then.'

Angie was about to defend his mother with some soothing platitude but decided not to. She hadn't liked the woman—had despised her, in fact—and didn't blame Lance one iota for feeling the way he did. She'd been a cold and unloving mother, and, it seemed, a miserable wife—a beautiful but cold bitch, whose priorities in life were money and social status.

'I see,' was all she said, which brought another sharp look.

'Yes, you would,' Lance said, admiration in his voice. 'Any other woman would have made some inanely sympathetic remark and not meant a single word of it. But not you, Angie. You're your mother's daughter. Straight down the line. You've no idea how much I appreciate that. A man would always know where he stood with you. There'd be no deceptions. No lies. No bull.'

She felt warmed by his compliments, yet perturbed at the same time. What she wanted was the same from Lance. No deceptions. No lies. No bull. Ever!

'Then tell me what you do, Lance,' she insisted. 'Give me a run-down of a typical day in the life of Lance Sterling. Or, better still, a typical week.'

He slid a wry smile her way. 'Ah, that sounds like Angie Brown, psychologist and counsellor, taking over. This *is* the way you people get to know your patients, isn't it? By getting them to tell you about themselves. Maybe we should pull over and I could lie down in the back seat and pretend it's a couch.'

'And maybe you should just keep driving and answer my questions.'

He sighed. 'You might not like the answers.'

'I'll risk it.'

She didn't like the answers at all. She was appalled by them. Lance's normal daily schedule was horrendous. He worked eighteen-hour days during the week, with little time for anything else. Then, at the weekend, he seemed to be still working, even when he was playing golf or going to dinner or the theatre. They were business rather than social engagements. She began to appreciate where his marriage might have gone wrong. And said so.

'Ah, but you forget,' he argued back. 'For the first three years of my marriage I didn't hold this gruelling position. I had plenty of time for my marriage, and my wife. For the first two years whenever I went overseas Helen went with me.'

Angie ignored the stab of jealousy this evoked to concentrate on the facts Lance was relaying.

'By the time my father died, my marriage was already on the rocks. Helen was refusing to accompany me just about everywhere. She'd started refusing to sleep with me. She lived her own life and went her own way.'

'I must be honest, Lance,' Angie said painfully. 'Your present lifestyle is not conducive to a happy family life, even if your wife loved you.'

'Is this still Angie the counsellor speaking? Or Angie the woman considering my proposal of marriage?'

'Both.'

'So you see no hope for us, if I continue as managing director of Sterling Industries?'

'I . . . I won't marry that man,' she stated bravely. And meant it.

Lance must have heard the conviction in her voice, for he swore under his breath. 'Would you become that man's mistress?' he asked brusquely, slanting her a narrow-eyed look.

Angie had never felt so dismayed in all her life. Or more disappointed. She should have known that this would be Lance's next move. His aim, after all, was not so much to install her as his loving wife, but as a permanent bed-partner.

'Well?' he persisted harshly. 'Would you?'

Angie gulped. 'Yes, I probably would,' she confessed with a bitter honesty. But she refused to meet his eyes. She felt too ashamed.

For being a man's mistress was based on lust, not love. It wasn't a real relationship. Lance was offering her sex, and nothing more. Love didn't come into it.

Yet it was love which would propel her into such a role. A love which refused to die. A love which could make her untrue to herself, and the values she had been brought up with.

The most awful silence descended on the car.

Angie kept her head turned away from him and the miles flew past. They stopped only once, and briefly. Lance drove on and on—not speeding, but pushing the car to the limit all the time. The countryside grew browner, and Angie saw first-hand the drought that her father had been complaining about all year.

A good farmer, Morris Brown had made enough money to send both his children to university in Sydney, but while he could protect his crops from disease there was little he could do about the lack of rain. Luckily the Brown farm was bounded on one side by a river, but even that was down to a trickle in parts.

Not that her father would be worrying about drought at this moment, Angie conceded unhappily. His mind would be on other worries. As were her own.

'Am I to take you home?' Lance asked at last as they came into the main street of Wilga, which was fairly deserted at noon on a hot December Sunday. 'Or do you want to go straight to the hospital?'

'To the hospital. There might not be anyone at home.'

'Which way, then?'

Angie gave him directions and soon he was parking his car in the hospital car park. The heat blasted Angie as she opened the door, a testimony to the car's excellent air-conditioning. Thankfully, the hospital was air-conditioned as well.

It was a fairly modern building, extensions and renovations having been made only two years ago—not so much because the town of Wilga was growing, but because the hospital had to service a large area. Recent government cutbacks had forced several smaller hospitals and clinics in adjoining towns to close, which meant that patients were sent to the Wilga hospital from up to a hundred miles away.

'There's Bud's car,' Angie pointed out on their way through the car park. 'Oh, and there's Dad's utility!' She wasn't sure if this was good news or bad. Were they all at the hospital because her mother was still deathly ill? Or because she was better and they could talk to her? Either way, it did seem likely that Nora was still alive. Angie desperately hoped so.

Lance placed a supportive hand on her shoulder as they pushed through the heavy glass doors which led into Reception. 'She's a fighter, your mum,' he said soothingly. 'She'll be all right.'

But Angie was worried. Even if her mother pulled through this attack, she could see further health problems down the road. The doctor had told her mother years ago to lose weight because of her high blood pressure, but Nora hadn't seemed able to give up the rich foods she loved. Angie had no doubt

that this had been a contributory factor in her
mother's coronary. She also doubted whether Nora
would take a blind bit of notice if told to go on a
special low-fat diet.

Her voice was shaking when she asked the woman
behind the reception desk about her mother. 'Mrs
Nora Brown,' Angie repeated. 'She . . . she had a
heart attack. I'm her daughter. From Sydney.'

The woman's smile brought some welcome re-
assurance. 'Oh, yes. I had your brother and father
in here not long ago. Mrs Brown's been moved from
Intensive Care to a general ward so I think you can
take that as good news. She's in Ward C, room ten.
You take the lifts over there to level three, turn right
and follow the signs.'

Angie almost burst into tears with relief.
Somehow, she held on, but her 'thank you' was
choked out, and she was blinking madly as she
hurried over to the lifts.

Room ten in Ward C was a private room, though
small. When Angie went in, her mother appeared
to be asleep, lying grey-faced in the white hospital
bed. Angie's father was sitting by her side, holding
her hand. Bud was standing at the small window,
looking out at the limp trees beyond. Both men's
eyes snapped up to hers as she entered, her father's
brightening, Bud's still full of reproach.

'Angie's here,' Morris Brown whispered excitedly to his wife, and her eyes shot open.

'Angie,' her mother rasped, in a voice so hoarse
and shaky that Angie almost broke down. When
her mother held out her hands to her, she suc-

cumbed to those long-threatening tears and threw herself into her mother's arms.

'There, there, Angie, love,' her mother crooned, stroking her daughter's hair. 'I'm all right. It'd take more than a silly old heart flutter to kill me.'

'Heart flutter, my foot,' her husband rebuked, but gently. 'You'd have been as dead as a doornail if I hadn't got you in here as quick as I did.'

'What an exaggerator your father is, Angie,' Nora said, lifting her daughter's tear-stained face up and wiping away the wetness with the bedsheet. 'All I had was a little clot stuck in the wrong place for a little while. The doc says the ECG shows no lasting damage.'

'The doc also said that if she doesn't take herself in hand where her diet is concerned she might not be so lucky the next time.'

'Diet, diet, diet,' Nora sighed. 'That's all I've been hearing about ever since I woke up. I think diet is the most offensive four-letter word ever invented.'

' "Dead" is worse,' Bud grumbled. 'For pity's sake, Mum, you have to do what the doctor said. Diet does not mean starve. It means eating different things, that's all.'

'Oh, piffle!' she scorned.

'So that's where she got that word from,' Lance muttered, from where he was standing just inside the room.

Nora Brown's eyes turned to him for the first time. 'Well, Lord be praised, if I didn't know better

I'd think that was Lance Sterling over there! Angie, tell me I'm not seeing things.'

Angie sat up straight and threw a wry smile over her shoulder at Lance. 'I wish I could, Mum, but I'm afraid you're quite right. It is Lance. He turned up at Bud's birthday party on Friday night, like the proverbial bad penny, and was still in Sydney when the news about you came through. He was kind enough to drive me up here.'

Angie watched the wheels in her mother's intuitive head start going round, but she was darned if she was going to explain how Lance had come to be on the spot in the early hours of this morning.

'Well, well,' was all her mother said, but it spoke volumes to anyone who knew her. She stared at Lance, then at a suddenly blushing Angie, then back at Lance again. 'That was extraordinarily kind of you, Lance. Now, come over here, you handsome hunk, and give your second-best girlfriend a hug.'

Lance laughed, then did just that. 'Hello, Mrs Brown,' he greeted her warmly. 'Glad to see you haven't changed.'

'Can't say the same for you, my lad. You look mighty peaky. What you need is a good night's sleep and some fresh country air. Why don't you stay up here at the farm with Dad for a while?'

'I'd love to, Mrs Brown, but I have urgent business back in Melbourne to attend to tomorrow, which really can't wait. I'll have to drive back to Sydney first thing tomorrow morning, then take a plane.'

Angie contemplated telling her parents about the death of Lance's father, then decided it was hardly the time or the place.

'Pity,' Nora said. 'You young people don't know how short life is. Don't waste the one you have doing things that don't make you happy. And don't keep putting off doing the things you know you should have done years ago.'

Angie might have imagined it, but she thought her mother was directing a definite message at Lance with those last words.

'Scares like the one I've just had rather make one reassess life,' she went on. 'Dad and I have decided to go on that holiday we've been putting off for years—haven't we, Dad?'

'We certainly have, Mother. Hang the expense. *And* the overdraft.'

A hatchet-faced nurse with a bosom like the bridge on a battleship bustled in at that moment and ordered all visitors out, putting paid to any more conversation about holidays or wasted lives.

'Doctor says Mrs Brown is to rest,' Sister Sour-puss stated firmly when Angie's dad objected. 'And that includes you, Mr Brown. You need some rest as well.'

'The chooks and dogs need feeding anyway,' Nora reminded him. 'I'll see you tonight, perhaps?' she said, looking at Sour-puss for permission.

That gesture alone showed just how much this attack had dented Nora's confidence. She normally never looked for permission to do anything from anyone. Still, old Sour-puss would have a deflating effect on just about anyone, Angie thought.

'I suppose you can have visitors tonight,' came the grudging concession. 'But only for an hour or so.'

Angie hated saying goodbye after so little time. Neither did she like leaving her mother in the hands of such a tyrant, but she could see the sense in her mother resting. Her father looked tired too. Wrecked, in fact. No doubt he hadn't eaten properly since her mother's attack and might need looking after himself.

She decided then and there not to go back to Sydney with Lance in the morning. She would stay and look after her father for a while. The school wouldn't fall apart at this time of the year if she had a week off—all the Year Twelve students had already left, and in two weeks the summer break would begin.

She would probably have to return the following week to tidy things up. And, given the situation with Lance, she might even have to hand in her resignation. She assumed that becoming his mistress would necessitate a move to Melbourne. Much as she didn't want to move to Melbourne to live, she'd passed the point where such considerations mattered. She would go wherever Lance was, to be with him as much as possible. End of story.

'Why don't you take Dad home, Bud?' she suggested to her brother as they all walked along the hospital corridor. 'Lance and I'll buy some take-away food and follow you as quickly as we can.'

'Fair enough,' came his curt reply. 'Get plenty of it, though. I'm damned hungry.' He stalked off, his body language telling its own story. Clearly they were not yet forgiven for the horrendous transgression of becoming lovers.

'I'll talk to him,' Lance said.

Angie sighed and shook her head. 'I doubt it will do any good. He's very angry with me.'

'No. He's very angry with *me*. And with good reason.'

She halted, her head snapping round to stare up at him with questioning eyes.

'That summer,' he explained with a weary sigh, 'after we got back to uni, Bud had some photos developed that he'd taken of all of us during my stay at the farm. They showed in living colour what he hadn't noticed in the flesh; that you and I had...feelings...for each other. He accused me of having already seduced you. I assured him that I hadn't, but he still went right off his brain. He told me if I ever touched you he'd kill me. He pointed out how young you were, and how innocent. He made me see you deserved a whole lot better than a cad and a spoiled bastard like me. Frankly, Angie, I agreed with him. I still do. And so do you. That's why you won't marry me.'

Angie was shaking her head and trying not to cry. So that was what had happened all those years ago...

'But I'm not as bad as Bud's made me out to be,' Lance added ruefully. 'I think I might even be redeemable. I just hope it's not too late.'

Angie looked up at him again, frowning her confusion at his cryptic remarks. 'Too late for what?'

'Too late to win what I want,' he said seductively, the brilliant blue of his eyes darkening as they caressed her. 'You, Angie. I want you . . .' And his mouth bent to hers.

She flinched back from his kiss in the end, frightened by his growing sexual power over her. For she wanted him back—right now and in the most basic way. How could she possibly want him like that? *Here*, of all places, with her mother lying ill down the hallway, and with his giving her nothing but bewildering and probably hollow promises about redeeming himself.

What kind of redemption was there for a man like him? she thought savagely. He was still going back to Melbourne tomorrow. In the end, any feelings he had for her weren't strong enough to keep him here, by her side.

No doubt he would send for her. Till she could move down there permanently there would be plane tickets and hotel reservations for romantic weekend rendezvous. And, weak fool that she was, she would fly to him and let him use her shamelessly. She actually felt perversely excited by the prospect.

Her laugh carried both nerves and a bitter acceptance of her own folly. 'Then you've got what you want, Lance. I've already agreed to become your lover.' She refused to use the word 'mistress', which had connotations she did not like. It was too removed from love, sounding like a business arrangement rather than a personal one.

'An agreement I will never let you back away from,' he ground out, pulling her into his arms. 'No matter what.'

His kiss, this time, allowed no room for escape. It dominated and devoured, giving her a further taste of what was to come. She was trembling inside by the time he let her go, and it wasn't all from desire.

Dear God, what had she done, becoming involved with Lance like this? She might not have told him in so many words that she loved him but he knew it. Everything he did and said betrayed that knowledge. She wanted to scream, but instead she wound her arms up around his neck and pulled his mouth back down on hers, kissing him as violently and possessively as he had kissed her. When she finally wrenched her mouth away, her heart and head were pounding.

'Don't go thinking my agreeing to be your lover is a licence to treat me badly, Lance,' she bit out breathlessly. 'I will have your respect, or you can go to hell!'

'If I ever fail to respect you, my darling, I'll willingly go there myself!'

Angie was taken aback by the fierceness of his vow. If she'd been a complete fool, she might almost have thought he truly loved her. Common sense, however, told her that Lance didn't have the capacity for that kind of love. He'd never grown up with it and had married without it. His wanting her didn't mean that he loved her.

But she could pretend, couldn't she? Pretend he loved her as much as she loved him. He did care for her, in his way. And he did want her. That much she could attest to. If last night was anything to go by, he wanted her one heck of a lot!

Thinking about sex had a very agitating effect on her, and she whirled to set off down the corridor.

Lance was hot on her heels. 'I take it we're off to buy some food. Or are we looking for somewhere private?' he added on a drily amused note.

Colour zoomed into her cheeks as she ground to a halt and glared up at him, her mouth opening, ready to reel off a ream of castigating words. But as she looked up into his face suddenly all she could see was that wickedly sexy mouth, all she could think about were the wicked delights that mouth could deliver.

Self-disgust at her wayward thoughts had her eyes and mouth hardening. 'Don't go letting that kiss go to your head, Lance. Or anywhere else for that matter. I was merely making a point!'

'And you made it very well, too,' he returned with a twisted grimace.

'Then stop being provocative.'

'I wasn't trying to be. I thought a touch of humour might defuse some of the tension flying around here.'

'Well, it hasn't!'

'Yes, I can see that.'

'I'm beginning to wish you hadn't brought me up here.'

'I can see that too.'

'I don't want you kissing me any more. Not up here.'

'I don't want you kissing me, either. It's too bloody uncomfortable.'

'I won't. Don't worry.'

'Good. Let's go, then.'

Angie ground her teeth when he took off and she practically had to run to keep up with him. 'Slow down,' she grumbled.

'Sorry. There isn't time. I've wasted too much as it is.'

He surged on ahead again and she raced on after him, her thoughts whirling. Wasted it on me, does he mean?

Angie would have asked him, but his expression forbade her asking. Besides, she might not like the answer. She made a decision there and then not to ask Lance too many questions about anything. She had a feeling that she would never like the answers he'd give her, or the lies he might be forced to tell.

CHAPTER TWELVE

'MR BROWN...'

Everyone looked up from their plates when Lance spoke. They'd been seated at the kitchen table for a full ten minutes, eating their fill of the take-away food Lance and Angie had brought back to the farm.

No one had said much, everyone seeming to have private thoughts as they munched away on fried chicken, chips and fresh bread rolls. Angie was extremely irritated with Bud, who kept giving her and Lance scowling looks which would have raised considerable questions in her father if he hadn't been so distracted.

'Yes, Lance?' Morris Brown said.

'About that holiday you and Mrs Brown are planning...'

'Yes, what about it?'

'I know you're a proud man, and would never accept charity, but it would give me great pleasure to give you that holiday. Please look upon it as a thank-you for the kindness you and Mrs Brown showed me when I stayed here that summer all those years ago. It was the best holiday I've ever had, and I've never forgotten it.'

Bud made some kind of snorting sound, which brought a startled look from his father and a black glare from Angie.

'You don't think I should take Lance's offer?' Morris asked his son in a puzzled tone.

Angie sent her brother a pleading look and he relented, if a little ungraciously. 'Of course you should. He can afford it—can't you, Lance?' he added, clapping Lance around the shoulders in a pretend buddy-buddy gesture. 'A few grand is a mere drop in the ocean to a Sterling.'

Morris shook his head. 'That's not the point. It's very kind of you, Lance, but I'm not sure Mother would like the idea. She doesn't like being beholden to people. She's never been keen on expensive presents, either.'

Angie reached out to cover her father's hand with hers. 'Dad, don't be silly. As Lance said, you and Mum gave him a free holiday, and now he's giving you one back.'

'I suppose so,' he sighed. 'But nothing too expensive, mind. And not too much travelling. Somewhere here in Australia. Somewhere really beautiful and peaceful.'

'I know just the place,' Lance said. 'Orpheus Island. It's one of the most northern and most beautiful of the Barrier Reef Islands, but also one of the most private.'

And one of the most expensive, Angie thought, but kept her mouth shut. Bud didn't say a word either, thank heavens, though his dark eyebrows arched in a way which suggested that he knew what a stay on Orpheus Island would cost.

'Mother's always wanted a holiday on one of those islands,' Morris mused.

'Then she shall have one,' Lance pronounced firmly. 'Angie, if I give you the money will you organise it? I think around May next year would be best. Your mum will be feeling up to it by then, and the weather up there is great at that time of the year.'

Angie heard the first-hand experience in his voice and was reminded once again of the difference between their lifestyles. Lance had always been able to indulge whatever whim or fancy came his way— which included jetting off to all the exclusive romantic hideaways in the world. Who knew? Maybe she was just his latest whim or fancy?

'May would be good,' Morris agreed. 'I'll have picked the summer crops by then. And the neighbours would look after the animals for us.'

'That's settled, then,' Lance said, sounding pleased.

Morris scraped back his chair and stood up. 'If you young 'uns don't mind, I think I'll go for a walk down to the river. I have a damned awful headache and that usually clears it. I won't be too long.'

Angie watched her father's dejected stoop as he pushed open the screen door and stepped out on to the side veranda. She hoped her mother was genuinely on the way to a full recovery because

Morris Brown just wouldn't be the same without her. They shared that kind of love.

'It must be nice to be able to buy whatever you want,' Bud said nastily, his small dark eyes gleaming at Lance with a bitter enmity. 'Friendship. Approval. *My Sister*! God, Angie, haven't you got any pride? Don't you know that you're only one of hundreds? When he grows bored with screwing you he'll toss you aside like a used tissue. You're nothing to him but a challenge, because you're the only female he didn't sleep with at the time of first fancying you. And now you're no longer a challenge. You're just another silly little fool who couldn't wait to get her pants off for the great Lance Sterling!'

'That's enough!' Lance snapped, spreading his hands out on either side of his plate and levering himself to his feet.

Suddenly Angie was afraid. She'd never seen Lance look so threatening, or so furious. She dimly recalled Bud telling her that Lance had dabbled in many sports back in his uni days, including the martial arts. With his naturally athletic physique he wouldn't need to recall too many of those skills to make mincemeat out of Bud if he chose to.

'Outside, Bud,' he bit out.

'Lance, no!' Her cry sent those blazing blue eyes flashing to her. 'Please don't,' she pleaded.

'I'm not challenging your brother to a duel, Angie. I simply want to straighten out some things.'

'Are . . . are you sure?'

'For Pete's sake, Angie!' Bud exploded irritably. 'We're adult men, not children. Besides, I can bloody well look after myself. I don't need my kid sister to come to my aid. If Lance wants to shove my teeth down my throat, then let him try. A lot of water's gone under the bridge since he was the super athlete of Sydney Uni. I can hold my own these days, in more ways than one. I'm certainly no longer the easily impressed country yokel who was only too happy to lick Lance's boots in the old days.'

Angie shook her head at her brother but said nothing. If he didn't watch it, his teeth *would* get shoved down his throat. Fear filled her heart as she watched her brother and her lover stalk out into the yard, then over into the barn, shutting the doors behind them. She rather expected to see the walls shaking and dust flying out from under them, as one saw in cartoons, but all remained ominously silent for a good twenty minutes, then the doors slowly opened.

They emerged together, Bud looking a little stunned but none the worse for wear. He wandered off in the direction of the river while Lance whirled and strode back towards the house. Angie raced out to meet him on the front veranda.

'What happened?' she burst out. 'What did you say to him?'

He stared at her for a few excruciatingly long and tense moments, before answering, 'That's between Bud and me, Angie.'

'But... but...'

'Don't try to pry it out of Bud, either,' he interrupted curtly. 'It'll put him in a very awkward position. Look, I've decided to drive back to Sydney straight away, Angie. The sooner I get back to Melbourne, the better. That way I should be able to return to Sydney by next weekend. What are your plans regarding your mother? How long will you be staying up here?'

Angie's head was whirling. She wasn't at all sure what was going on. 'I . . . I thought I'd stay at least a week.'

'So you won't be back in Sydney next weekend?'

'No. I dare say Bud will have gone back by then, but I thought I'd take the Sunday night train back. I really will have to be back at school for the last week of the term. Lance, what's going on?'

'What do you mean? Are you still talking about what happened between Bud and me?'

'No, I'm talking about *you* and me. What is it you want of me, Lance? What do you expect?'

'Are you going back on what you agreed in the car on the way up here?' he demanded, blue eyes immediately wary.

Her chin lifted even while her heart contracted. 'No. I'm not.'

His triumphant expression unnerved her, as did the way his eyes slid down her body then up again. 'You know what *I* want, Angie, but I'm not quite sure what to expect from *you*. Yet. Time will tell, though. I'm a patient man.'

'Stop talking in riddles!' she snapped. 'You know I hate that kind of thing. Spell it out for me. Are you planning on flying up to Sydney for dirty weekends? Or do you expect me to resign and move to Melbourne? Don't go thinking you'll set me up in some sleazy flat somewhere. I won't stand for that kind of hole-and-corner relationship. If I'm to be your girlfriend, it will be a normal man-woman relationship, nothing nasty. I pay my own way and you pay yours.'

He whistled at her tough stance. 'That's my Angie! All right, I'll tell you all I can for now. I don't expect you to resign and move to Melbourne. *I'm* going to move to Sydney, as soon as that can be arranged. You can stay living exactly where you are and working where you are . . . for the time being.'

Delight raced through Angie. And relief. Tears of happiness danced in her eyes. 'I can? Oh, Lance, that's wonderful! Oh, you've made me so happy.'

He said nothing for a moment, merely stared at her. Then he took her in his arms and kissed her with a passion that sent tremors rippling through both of them.

'Tell me you love me,' he rasped against her swollen quivering mouth.

There was no hesitation this time, no thoughts of self-protection. 'I love you,' she said, her voice shaking.

'And you'll never love anyone else?'

'I never have and I never will.'

'That's all I need to know,' he ground out. 'What time will you get back to your flat after work on Monday week?'

'Around four-thirty.'

'I'll be there,' he said, and, whirling away from her, hurried down the steps and over to his car. He didn't look back at her, didn't say another word.

It wasn't till the black car was speeding off down the valley road that Angie realised one crucial thing. Lance had not said he loved her back.

CHAPTER THIRTEEN

'LANCE gone, has he?'

Angie looked up from where she was sitting on the front steps, her eyes dull with depression. 'Yes,' was all she could manage without bursting into tears.

It was some seconds before she realised that Bud was staring at her, a most peculiar look on his face. He seemed both astonished and puzzled, as though he was trying to see into her soul but without much success.

'Don't look at me like that, Bud,' she snapped. 'You don't understand. I love him. I've always loved him. Ever since that first summer. I know you don't think he's worthy of being loved like that, but he is. Down deep Lance is a fine man. You just don't understand him.'

He raised both his hands, as if to ward off the defensive daggers in her words. 'You're wrong there, Angie. I think I understand Lance very well. Maybe even better than you do.'

Angie jumped to her feet, her eyes spitting fire at her brother. 'God, not that superstud stuff again, Bud. That's ancient history. What is it with you, that you feel compelled to run Lance down all the time? You're supposed to be his best friend. Fine friend you turned out to be. You know what? I think you're jealous of him. I think you've always been jealous of him!'

Angie planted furious hands on her hips as Bud started looking her up and down, a stupid grin on his face. 'I think I'm beginning to see what Lance sees in you, Angie. You've turned into one hell of a fiery female! I guess I was stuck in a time-warp, still thinking of you as a quiet, shy little teenager— so innocent in the ways of the world, needing your big brother to protect you from wolves like Lance.'

'Lance is *not* a wolf!' she protested hotly. 'He wasn't back then, and he isn't now. You make it sound like he had to seduce me or something. I assure you he didn't. I was only too willing to be seduced!'

'So he said.'

'He did?' Angie frowned at this news. She didn't like the sound of it. 'What else did he say about me?' she demanded to know.

'I'm not at liberty to tell you.'

Disgruntlement curled her lips. 'What on earth does that mean? Why can't you tell me what he said? Why do you both have to be so damned se-cretive all of a sudden?'

'That's the way Lance wanted it.'

'Since when do you do what Lance says? I'm your sister, for heaven's sake. Your first loyalty is to me.'

Bud laughed. 'Really? Then you don't know anything about true mateship, do you?'

'Oh, piffle. You and Lance haven't been true mates for donkey's years.'

'Fat lot you know, little sister. Men aren't like women. They don't have to see each other every week for their friendship to remain solid. Lance and I sorted out a lot of things today, and we're better friends now than ever.'

Angie scowled at her brother. 'Well, bully for you!'

Bud laughed. 'I'd watch that language, if I were you, madam. Any woman gracing Lance Sterling's arm wouldn't be expected to go around tossing off Aussie slang all the time.'

'Is that so?' Angie said archly, infuriated at this about-face in Bud.

'Yes, that's so. He has a certain position to uphold, you know.'

'Well, stone the crows, Bud,' she drawled, in the broadest Aussie accent, 'maybe I should just grace his bed, then, and not his arm. I'm sure the almighty Lance Sterling won't care what language I come out with there. I reckon I could be as colourful as I like and he wouldn't object.'

Bud's face darkened. 'Cut it out, Angie.'

'Why should I? Now that you're back licking Lance's boots you might as well know the whole score. I don't know what Lance told you in that barn, but the truth is he asked me to marry him and I turned him down. I told him I wasn't prepared to be the wife of some high-powered wheeler-dealer who spent more time in the air than on the ground. Of course, Lance wasn't fazed one bit by my knocking back his proposal of marriage. He merely moved on to his next proposition to get me permanently into his bed. He asked me to be his mistress! How do you like dem apples?' she flung at him.

'Who's running Lance down now?'

'I'm entitled to. I'm the one who loves the bastard!'

He glared at her for several seconds before slowly shaking his head, a rueful smile splitting his round face. 'You know what, Angie? I almost pity Lance. All these years, I thought you needed protecting from him. But I was wrong. It's really the other way around. The poor bastard,' he said, chuckling as he walked away. 'Who would have believed it?'

A tap on Angie's office door sent her eyes to the wall clock. It was three thirty-five, a little early for Vanessa, who was a conscientious teacher and never dashed out of the classroom straight after the bell.

Angie rather wished Vanessa might be less conscientious today, with Lance coming to the flat at four-thirty. She hadn't heard from him since his departure from the farm over a week ago, either by letter or telephone—a situation she found unnerving. Yet, despite that, she had no doubt he would turn up today, as he had said he would.

'Come in,' she called, when the door-tapper didn't automatically enter.

It was Debbie, looking sheepish but happy. 'Sorry to bother you, Miss,' she said, hovering in the doorway. 'I know I don't have an appointment but I just wanted you to know I... I didn't do it. You know... with Warren. I thought about what you said and I decided to wait till someone more special came along.'

Angie's eyes misted before she could stop them.

'I also wanted to ask if you'll be here next year...' Debbie blathered on, God bless her. 'I mean ... you're the third counsellor we've had in three years, and they all seem to leave after a year. We all like you a lot, Miss, and think you're real cool. Even Gloria likes you!'

Angie had to laugh, for she knew what Debbie meant. Gloria was the meanest, toughest, bitchiest girl in the whole school.

'That certainly is a true compliment,' Angie said, green eyes gleaming, but with laughter now, not tears. 'Yes, Debbie, I'll still be here next year.'

'Gosh, that's great. I'll tell all the others. We thought, after you were away last week, that you might have been getting sick of us, and took time off to look for another job.'

'No, it wasn't anything like that. My mum was ill. She had a heart attack. But she's getting better now. In fact, she came home from hospital yesterday.'

'Gee, Miss, we didn't know. No one told us,' Debbie said, resentment pursing her pretty young mouth. 'No one tells us anything! If we'd known we'd have bought a card or something. It's not as though we don't care.'

Angie felt warmed by the girl's sentiments. Moments like this made what she did worthwhile.

'I know you care, Debbie,' she said, a lump filling her throat. 'And I'm so proud of you for the decision you made. It was a very mature one.'

Debbie grinned. 'Yeah. I thought so too. But don't tell anyone else. I lied my teeth out and said sex was fantastic!'

Vanessa popped her head in the door moments after Debbie had disappeared. 'What did that little raver want?' she said scornfully. 'Do you know she's been going round telling everyone she lost her cherry last weekend? What kind of girls are parents bringing up these days? I ask you!'

'Not a very different kind from our generation,' Angie said wryly. 'We all struggle along, trying to work out what sex and love are all about, and we all make the most horrendous mistakes.'

Vanessa's dark eyes narrowed suspiciously. 'Are you saying you made a mistake becoming involved with lover-boy again?'

Angie stood up and began tidying her desk. 'Of course. He won't ever give me what I want, Vanessa.'

'Which is?'

'A normal family life, with a house and kids, and a hubbie who comes home every night.'

'Yuk! Give me penthouse suites and wild orgies and private jets any day.'

'You fibber! I saw the way you were batting your eyelashes at Bret Johnson today. And you couldn't get a more normal, down-to-earth bloke. So what's going on between you and the economics teacher?'

'Not much. Yet,' Vanessa added with a wicked grin. 'But he likes me. He *really* likes me.'

'And why not? You're very likeable...for a feminist and a maths teacher. You can tell me all about him on the way home. It'll keep my mind off Lance.'

'Nothing,' Vanessa said drily, 'is going to keep your mind off him, love. You know it and I know it.'

Angie groaned. 'You could be right.'

CHAPTER FOURTEEN

THE sight of Lance's black Audi already parked outside their block of flats showed Angie that her confidence in his turning up today had all been a sham. Underneath, she'd been terrified he wouldn't.

'Hey, watch it!' Vanessa warned her sharply, when the car drifted dangerously close to a van going the other way.

'Sorry. I was distracted there for a second.'

'Yes, I can see myself what caused it. I thought you said he wasn't due till four-thirty,' Vanessa finished drily.

'That . . . that's what he told me.' Angie did her best to control her shaking hands, voice and insides, but without much success.

'Well, it's only twenty-three minutes past four. He seems keen, Angie.'

'Yes, but for what?'

Vanessa's head whipped round, her dark eyebrows arching. 'My, my—I thought I was the only cynic around here.'

Angie sighed. 'I'm fast catching up.'

'Men do that to you. Especially men who look like that.'

Both women watched Lance emerging from his car as they drove down the street towards him. He was casually dressed this time, in blue jeans and a

175

navy short-sleeved golf shirt with a crisp red stripe
around the open-necked collar. Despite his everyday
clothes, he still managed to look rich and perversely glamorous. Maybe it was that gorgeous hair
of his, glinting gold in the sun, or the gleam of real
gold on his wrist and fingers. Or maybe it was just
the way he carried himself.

Were wealthy men born with that air of lazy arrogance? Angie wondered. Or did it just develop
over the years of being treated as superior beings?

Even Vanessa was shaking her head. 'That is
some man, Angie,' she said with rueful acceptance.
'I can understand why you flipped over him. If he
asked me to be his mistress, I'd say yes like a shot.
There again, I'd have agreed to be his wife. I have
to admire your strength of character in saying no,
there. Still, perhaps it's your saying no that's made
him so keen. I can't imagine too many women
saying no to him over the years.'

'Mmm,' was all Angie could say, her eyes locking
with Lance's as she slid the car into the kerb behind
him. 'Would you mind putting the car in the garage
for me, Vanessa?' she asked her flatmate. 'I'd like
to speak to Lance out here for a minute.'

'Spoilsport,' Vanessa grumbled.

'I'll bring him up for coffee shortly.'

'OK. I'll put the kettle on.'

Lance walked over to hold the car door open for
Angie as she swung her legs out, his gaze flicking
down then up her body as she did so. She couldn't
tell if he liked the way she looked or not; his expression was quite bland.

Her work image was a far cry from the glammed-up party look Lance had encountered the night of Bud's birthday, and from the way she'd been dressed the following day. She always wore simple suits and tailored blouses to school, which didn't stand out among the uniforms and didn't bring too much attention to her natural good looks. Make-up was kept to a minimum, her long hair brushed straight back and secured at the nape of her neck with a clip or bow.

Today she was wearing a fawn suit with a knife-pleated skirt and a blazer jacket with cream buttons. Her blouse was cream, and a tortoiseshell clip held her hair tidily in place. She never bothered to curl it for work, leaving it quite straight.

'Hello, Angie,' he said. 'Vanessa,' he added, nodding at her as she too climbed out and began walking around the car towards the driver's side.

'Lance,' Vanessa replied succinctly, smiling a wry smile. 'Your punctuality is impressive.'

He merely smiled, saying nothing. Angie felt the tension behind his smile, and immediately succumbed to all kinds of doubts and fears.

He's come to tell me that it's over between us, she panicked. That he's decided not to move to Sydney. That I'm more trouble than I'm worth.

Yet if that was the case, logic argued back, why had he come in person? He would surely have chosen to give such bad news over the telephone, or by letter.

'Did…did you get all your business done?' Angie asked, once Vanessa had driven off and they were alone on the pavement.

'As much as was possible,' he returned cryptically. 'There are still some loose ends to tie up. But if you mean have I moved to Sydney to live,' he added, his eyes never leaving her worried face, 'I have.'

Her relief seemed to please him. But it didn't please herself. God, but she was hopeless. She might as well just serve herself up to him on a silver platter if she meant to go on like this, with an attached note which said, 'To be used and disposed of as you please!'

Love and pride were bad bedfellows, she decided unhappily. They made fools of each other.

'Would you like to come up for some coffee? Vanessa's going to put on the kettle.'

'I'd rather not, Angie. I'd like to talk to you alone,' he said, with a seriousness that sent those doubts and fears churning in her stomach again. 'Is there somewhere we could drive to? Some nearby park?'

'I . . . I suppose so. Let me just run upstairs and tell Vanessa, or she'll think I'm terribly rude.'

She returned to find Lance already behind the wheel of his car. Under her directions they drove to a small reserve down on McMahon's Point, where there were several park benches on a grassy verge overlooking the harbour. It was a chilly spot during the winter months, but on a warm sum-

mer's afternoon it was a delight, with a cooling
breeze and a view to soothe even the most troubled
heart.

And Angie's heart *was* troubled—so troubled
that she found it hard to keep silent while they
walked together towards the only vacant bench.
When they finally sank down upon the rather hard
wooden slats she immediately turned to face Lance.

'Lance, I...I'm not sure that I...that I——'

'Don't go on, Angie,' he cut in abruptly. 'Listen
to what I have to say first. Then you can have your
say.'

'All right.' She just knew she wasn't going to like
what he had to say.

'I haven't been strictly truthful with you.'

Angie's heart fell.

'I made a proposal to you that I had no intention
of going through with.'

Her heart fell even further.

'I just wanted to find out if you still loved me.
Once I did, believe me when I say I had no intention of letting you become my mistress. I had
no intention of letting you become anything but
my wife and the mother of my children.'

Angie's eyes flew up from where they'd dropped
to the ground.

Lance reached out to touch her cheek gently, and
her heart flipped over. 'I love you, Angie. I've
always loved you...ever since that summer...'

'But...but you never came back for me,' she
cried. 'And you married someone else!'

He shook his head, his hand falling from her cheek down into his lap. 'I foolishly allowed other forces to shape the course of my life. I thought I was being cruel to be kind. I thought I was unworthy of you.'

'How could you think that?' she groaned.

'Oh, Angie, Angie, have you any idea how different your family is from mine? That summer... I was given a taste of something so alien to everything I had ever known, something so damned wonderful that it ate me up with longing and envy.

'I'd already had an advance taste of the Browns with Bud, who was more openly honest and full of the love of life than any person I had ever met before. He was his own man, and I liked that. There were no pretensions about him, or airs and graces, as your mother would have said. He took me for what I was, not for what my parents owned. He liked nothing better than to bring me down a peg or two—a tendency he's perhaps taken too far over the years,' he added with a touch of acid.

'But truthfully,' Lance went on, reaching over to take her two hands in his, 'I could understand Bud's outrage where you were concerned. What brother would have wanted the man I was then for his fifteen-year-old sister? Hell, I wasn't really a man— I was nothing but a spoiled, arrogant, sex-crazed idiot, whose only feelings for girls up till then had resided firmly between my legs.

'It was so easy after I left the farm to tell myself I'd imagined those other feelings you engendered in me, to confuse the beginnings of a real love with the stirrings of lust, to excuse *your* feelings as little more than a schoolgirl crush which would fade in time.'

'I tried telling myself that as well,' Angie said, a sob catching in her throat. 'But I simply could not forget you.'

'Or I you. Though I tried damned hard. I avoided all girls who looked even remotely like you. Yet at the same time I was obviously looking for the kind of relationship you'd promised. When I first met Helen, she cleverly worked out what I wanted in a woman and played the part to the hilt. She convinced me that she wanted nothing but to be my wife and the mother of my children.

'It was all an act, of course. She came from a family who'd had money once but whose fortunes had declined after the property market crashed in the eighties. She married me for my money, and my money is all she got.

'I must take some blame for her subsequent behaviour, because it must have quickly become obvious to her that I loved her no more than she loved me. I did my best to make a go of the marriage but it was doomed from the start. After a few months of Helen refusing to sleep with me I hired that private detective, and put the final denouement into motion.'

'And it was during this time that you slept with someone else?' she asked carefully, needing to know the answer. 'Or were there a lot of women, Lance?'

'No, only one. Believe me when I tell you it meant nothing, Angie—either to me or to her. She was a hard-nosed career-woman in her mid-thirties. We met through business and she made it perfectly obvious that she was available. She used sex to de-stress her life, she said. I didn't much care what her motives were as long as she gave me what I wanted.

'That week, after Helen left, I finally took stock of my life. I looked at myself in the mirror and decided I did not like what I saw. Then I looked at something else, and I'm not ashamed to admit it, Angie—I cried.'

Angie's heart went out to him. 'What did you look at, Lance?'

'This, Angie...'

She sat, intrigued, as he drew his wallet out of his back pocket and extracted a folded and rather battered piece of paper. With careful and oddly tender movements he unfolded it and handed it over to her. Angie's breath caught as she realised what it was, the printed words leaping out at her from the page.

'It's my poem,' she choked out, her eyes blurring. 'The one I gave you that night...' She looked up at him through wet lashes. 'You kept it... all these years?'

'How could I ever throw it away? No one had ever loved me like that, Angie, or written me any-thing so beautiful. When I read it again that morning I couldn't contain my despair. But then slowly, over the next few days, my despair gradually turned to determination. I decided if there was even the slimmest chance for us I would take it.

'I knew you weren't married. I hoped and prayed you still felt something for me. It took me a few days to screw up the courage to actually act—Bud's birthday being the catalyst. I knew Bud's habit of always having a party, and I knew you'd be there.'

'So when you came to Bud's party... you really were coming for me at long last?'

'Yes,' he confessed, and Angie's heart swelled with happiness. 'One part of my mind kept telling me I was being an optimistic fool to pursue you after all these years. But once the idea took hold, I couldn't seem to rid myself of it.'

He smiled a drily amused smile. 'Of course, I still had a rather old picture of you in my mind. You've no idea of the shock I got when you answered the door that night. You rather dashed my hopelessly arrogant hopes in one fell swoop. This ravishing creature, I immediately realised, had not been waiting for yours truly to arrive on her doorstep. She certainly hadn't been pining for some old lost love in any way, shape or form.'

'But I had, Lance,' she cried, clasping the poem to her chest and looking at him with all the love in her heart. 'Truly.'

'Yes, I know, my love, and that's why I've done what I've done. I would move heaven and earth to make your dream come true, Angie, because it's my dream as well. I only hope it's enough.'

'What? What have you done?'

'Three things. I've resigned my position as acting managing director of Sterling Industries. I've put my house in Melbourne on the market, and I'm going into business with Bud up here in Sydney.'

Angie's mouth dropped open with shock.

'It's not such a huge sacrifice on my part,' he insisted. 'And I will not regret it later. With Dad dead and Mum gone, I have few feelings left for the family business. I've hired good people to run the various companies, and I can keep a general eye on proceedings from up here without it taking up much time. I might have to attend a few meetings a year. That's all.

'As far as my marital home is concerned...I don't have any fond memories there. I'll be only too happy to buy a new place up here. And as for going into business with Bud...I've always fancied myself doing something creative, and I think I'd be good at it. Bud told me the night of his party that he would start up an agency of his own if he could find a backer, so when we were speaking that day in the barn I proposed we go into business together, with my money and his expertise. Once he realised how serious I was about you, he agreed.'

Angie didn't know what to say. She was flummoxed and flabbergasted.

'Now I'm asking you again to marry me, Angie,' Lance said firmly. 'If you say yes, we'll go buy a :ng straight away. We won't be able to get married 'welve months, till my divorce comes through,

but meanwhile we can look for a house and plan
the sort of wedding your mum would want for you.

'If you say no, however, I won't give up. I'll do
everything in my power to get you to change your
mind. I'll pursue you, seduce you, even buy or
blackmail you if I have to. You will be my wife,
Angie Brown. Make no bones about it. So what's
it to be right at this moment? Yes? Or no again?'

Angie stared, first at Lance's handsome and im-
passioned face, then down at the poem she'd written
all those years ago. Not that she really needed to
read the words to remember its content. It was
firmly imprinted in her brain. But there was something incredibly moving about seeing them in their
original form—the large, simple print shouting out
the tender innocence of the poem's creator, the
battered piece of paper showing just how many
times Lance had unfolded this page to read them.

Every day I shall think of you -
Every night I shall dream of you -
One day you will come for me -
One night you'll be one with me -
Love burns eternal when it's true -
It does not die. I'll always love you.

'Angie?' Lance said, his voice husky. 'What's
your answer to be? Tell me, for pity's sake.'

She struggled for control as she looked up,
emotion welling up within her. She tried for a smile,
but she suspected she was crying.

'Yes,' she managed to get out, then suddenly broke into a dazzling smile. 'Yes, my darling. Oh, yes!'

And she threw herself into his arms.

* * * * *

If you enjoyed Angie and Lance's story, then look out for two more romances in Miranda Lee's beguiling new trilogy

AFFAIRS TO REMEMBER.

Coming next month:

A WEEKEND TO REMEMBER

When Jack Marshall loses his memory after an accident, his secretary Hannah knows just what she must do to protect him from the cunning clutches of a gold-digging actress: pretend to be his fiancée! Only once Hannah has become her boss's pretend lover, she doesn't want their fantasy weekend to end!

AFFAIRS TO REMEMBER: stories of love you'll treasure forever.

Merry Christmas, Baby!

A romantic collection filled with the magic
of Christmas and the joy of children.

SUSAN WIGGS, Karen Young and
Bobby Hutchinson bring you Christmas wishes,
weddings and romance, in a charming
trio of stories that will warm up your
holiday season.

MERRY CHRISTMAS, BABY! also contains
Harlequin's special gift to you—a set of
FREE GIFT TAGS included in every book.

Brighten up your holiday season with
MERRY CHRISTMAS, BABY!

Available in November at
your favorite retail store.

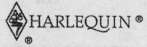

HARLEQUIN ®
®

Look us up on-line at: http://www.romance.net   MCB

Free Gift Offer

As Seen on TV!

With a Free Gift proof-of-purchase
from any Harlequin® book, you can receive
a beautiful cubic zirconia pendant.

This stunning marquise-shaped stone is a genuine cubic
zirconia—accented by an 18" gold tone necklace.
(Approximate retail value $19.95)

Send for yours today...
compliments of ◈HARLEQUIN®

To receive your free gift, a cubic zirconia pendant, send us one original proof-of-purchase, photocopies not accepted, from the back of any Harlequin Romance®, Harlequin Presents®, Harlequin Temptation®, Harlequin Superromance®, Harlequin Intrigue®, Harlequin American Romance®, or Harlequin Historicals® title available in August, September or October at your favorite retail outlet, together with the Free Gift Certificate, plus a check or money order for $1.65 u.s./$2.15 CAN. (do not send cash) to cover postage and handling, payable to Harlequin Free Gift Offer. We will send you the specified gift. Allow 6 to 8 weeks for delivery. Offer good until December 31, 1996, or while quantities last. Offer valid in the U.S. and Canada only.

Free Gift Certificate

Name: _____

Address: _____

City: _____ State/Province: _____ Zip/Postal Code: _____

Mail this certificate, one proof-of-purchase and a check or money order for postage and handling to: HARLEQUIN FREE GIFT OFFER 1996. In the U.S.: 3010 Walden Avenue, P.O. Box 9071, Buffalo NY 14269-9057. In Canada: P.O. Box 604, Fort Erie, Ontario L2Z 5X3.

The collection of the year!
NEW YORK TIMES BESTSELLING AUTHORS

Linda Lael Miller
Wild About Harry

Janet Dailey
Sweet Promise

Elizabeth Lowell
Reckless Love

Penny Jordan
Love's Choices

and featuring
Nora Roberts
The Calhoun Women

This special trade-size edition features four of the wildly
popular titles in the Calhoun miniseries together in
one volume—a true collector's item!

Pick up these great authors and a chance to win
a weekend for two in New York City at the
Marriott Marquis Hotel on Broadway! We'll pay
for your flight, your hotel—even a Broadway show!

Available in December at your favorite retail outlet.

NEW YORK
Marriott®
MARQUIS

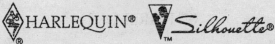

HARLEQUIN® ♥ *Silhouette*®

NYT1296-R

You're About to Become a

Become a

Privileged Woman

Reap the rewards of fabulous free gifts and benefits with proofs-of-purchase from Harlequin and Silhouette books

Pages & Privileges™

It's our way of thanking you for buying our books at your favorite retail stores.

✂

┌─────────────────────────┐
│ **PROOF OF**   │ HP-PP19
│ **PURCHASE**   │
│ Offer expires March 31,1997 │
└─────────────────────────┘

**Harlequin and Silhouette—
the most privileged readers in the world!**

For more information about Harlequin and Silhouette's PAGES & PRIVILEGES program call the Pages & Privileges Benefits Desk: **1-503-794-2499**

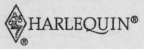

HARLEQUIN®